Hate to Love You

Ivy Symone

Chapter 1

I would be lying if I said I hadn't ever wished death on my husband. I was guilty. And I used to not feel bad about having those feelings. My husband was evil, and most days I hated him. I used to come up with outlandish schemes in my head to get rid of him without evidence coming back on me. I've watch *Snapped* many times. You had to play that shit careful, or a jury wouldn't believe your word.

Ironically, now that my husband Marcos Beauchamp was laid up in the hospital hanging on for dear life, I kind of felt guilty about my vindictive feelings. Did all of my hopeful wishes bring this about? I can't lie; a part of me was laughing inside. Not a giggle laugh either. It was one of those deep from the belly that worked its way up to the throat and came out forceful like you had heard the funniest shit ever. That's wrong; I know, but you don't understand. This man has taken me through hell, and it serves his ass right.

Four days before was our twin boys' sixteenth birthday. So, of course, we went all out for Bleu and Azul. We threw them a party that would definitely go down in their high school class as one of the best parties. Marcos booked some local rappers that I've never heard of who were affiliated with Cashville Records (Although once they started performing, I realized my sons have had me listening to them for quite a while). I left that kind of stuff up to Marcos. I focused on the decorations, food, and the big ass cake they had. The party was a blast. Our eighteen-year-old daughter Marcena was being salty because she said her sixteenth birthday celebration wasn't as good. I beg to differ.

In the middle of the party, I noticed I hadn't seen Marcos.

I asked everyone had they seen Marcos. Whenever his friends act evasively, I knew they were trying to cover for him. So I went searching for him.

The party was being held in the banquet hall of the Adele Beauchamp School of Music and Theatre. It was ours. Beverly Beauchamp was the acting CEO, President and Chief Instructor of the Adele Beauchamp School of Music and Theatre. The school was a nonprofit organization for low-income families providing quality theatre and music instructions to youth who otherwise wouldn't be able to afford it. Beverly was Marcos's mother, and Adele was Marcos's great-grandmother. It was the women in his life that got him and his siblings into the fine arts of dance, theatre, and music; therefore, when Beverly opened the school, she named the school after Adele in honor of her. The school has been running strong with a well-known reputation in the community for the past fifteen years.

After I earned my degree in Urban Studies with a minor in Nonprofit Management and Leadership, I wanted to come on board with the operations of the school. I was chief vice president and COO. I was actively involved with the program. Sometimes I think I was more passionate about the school than his mother was. Dancing and drama were more to me than a passion; it was an outlet. I used it to escape my sad life with Marcos.

Speaking of Marcos. My woman's intuition told me he was somewhere doing something he had no business doing. The first place I went to was the wing of administrative offices. I went from office to office in search of him. I didn't see him. With the loud music in the background, I stepped in the middle of the deserted atrium pondering on Marcos's whereabouts.

Then I heard it. Not it. *Them.* I heard *them.* Coming from one of the kids' lounge rooms. I slowly made my way toward the room. *Wasn't this some shit*? They didn't even have the decency to shut the door all the way. I stood at the door watching as Stacy pumped her pancake on Marcos's sausage. They were on the sofa. A sofa that the kids of the school had to sit on. That pissed me off.

Marcos held her around the small of her back as she rode him. He was saying something to her, but I couldn't make it out because it came out in whispering breaths. I stood there contemplating if I should yank Stacy off of him. What made it worse was that Stacy was an instructor there at the school. Needless to say, she no longer had a job now.

"Marcos," I spoke calmly. "When you're finished, can you please come back to the party. We're about to bring out the cake."

Stacy gasped and tried to jump off of his dick. Marcos held her still. He said to her, "Don't move." He glared at me like I was the one caught doing something wrong. "I'll be out there. Now get the fuck out."

I frowned at his lack of respect for me. I said, "Stacy...you're fired. And when you're done, you need to leave the party."

"I'm so sorry Neph—" she was trying to say. Marcos silenced her.

He looked at me. His facial expression softened as he began pumping his dick in and out of Stacy. I could tell she felt ashamed and her pale white skin had turned red. But it didn't stop her white ass from moaning.

Marcos continued to look at me as he got rougher with

her. A sinister smile spread across his face. *Sick bastard.* I hated him.

————

Later that night he got in bed after showering like nothing had happened. I stared at him. His muscular back was to me as he hugged his pillow pretending to be so tired. If I had a knife at that moment, I would have had to make a choice: stab him in the head or stab him in the back. I know! I would stab his ass straight in his butthole.

"Marcos?" I called softly.

"What Nephia?" he asked with an attitude.

"Why would you do that at your children's birthday party?" I asked.

"Man, leave me alone with that shit," he grumbled.

"It was disrespectful; to me and to the twins."

"Who saw me but you?"

"For real Marcos?" I asked in incredible disbelief.

He shifted in his spot but never turned around to face me. "Go head on with that shit Nephia. I ain't in the fuckin mood."

"How long have you been fucking her?" I wanted to know ignoring the warning tone of his voice.

He abruptly turned around and was on me so fast I didn't have time to react. I cowered under him blocking my face from any impending flying fists. He punched me upside my head and snarled, "Bitch, didn't I tell you don't fuck with me tonight?"

"Okay," I said weakly. I was always fine until the first blow. The first blow always weakened me and reminded me I was no match for him. It reminded me that I needed to shut the fuck up. Shit, Marcos was about two hundred pounds of rippling muscles. He stood right at five ten. I was five two at about a hundred and thirty. What could I do to him?

He hit me on top of my head again. "I'm getting tired of your bitch ass asking…," he hit me again, "mothafuckin questions!"

This is when I start to cry. I can see the fire in his eyes as his rage continue to grow. I shrink even more.

Marcos got out of the bed. "Fuck this shit! You always wanna see me angry and shit. I'm finna go and don't fuckin call me."

"Wait," I cried. "I'm sorry. I won't talk no more. I promise."

Pitiful huh? Yeah, I know.

"Fuck you Neph," he spat. He disappeared in our huge walk-in closet. I sat there crying softly. When he reappeared, he was fully dressed. He was still mad.

When he left the house, I knew where he was running to. And it wasn't to Stacy's. It was to his other baby mama's house Terra. She was another white girl who he had a nine-year-old daughter with. Her name was Brittani, and I liked the little girl. Her parents weren't worth shit, so when she did come over to the house, I treated her like she was my own.

Before he walked out of the room, he said under his breath, "Pitiful ass bitch."

That's what I was to him. A pitiful ass bitch. To others, I was a pitiful ass woman for putting up with his mess. I've been dealing with Marcos for nineteen years. Nineteen years of hell.

At 5:13 that morning I received a call from a frantic Terra. I couldn't make out anything she was saying. "Calm down! Now what?"

Terra tried to calm herself down. She was still sobbing. "It's Marcos. I think he ain't gon make it...He was in an accident."

"An accident?" I asked fully sitting up. "What are you talking about?"

"Marcos!"

I was hearing her right. I just didn't care. I said, "So why are you calling me?"

"You're his wife. You have to make decisions for him."

"I don't care what they do. He can die," I said carelessly.

"Marcos's right about you. You are a bitch!"

Fuck Marcos and his white bitch, I thought. Although Marcos referred to me as a bitch, I really wasn't. It's just some of the things that he had done caused me to behave outside my natural self. For instance: not caring about him. I wasn't a heartless person. As a matter of fact, I was too kind and understanding. I sighed, "What hospital?"

"Vanderbilt."

I ended the call with her. Did she say he might not make it? Was this my lucky day? I got up and quickly dressed. With my purse and keys in hand, I went to the twins' bedroom. I tapped Azul, "Zuli..."

He was so sleepy. They, meaning the twins and their five other friends sleeping over, probably had just gone to sleep. "Zuli, I'm leaving, but I'll be back."

"Where you go?" he asked.

"I'll call you," I told him. I wanted to wait to see how serious things were before alarming the kids.

"Okay," he said.

Bleu stirred in his sleep. "Where you going, Mama?"

"Go back to bed. Y'all look after the house until I get back."

When I arrived at the hospital, Terra was so distraught. She and Brittani were waiting in the emergency operating room waiting area for family and friends. She explained to me that she was notified because her number was the last few calls in Marcos's phone. That was all she was able to tell me before I was being pulled aside by the police that was called to the scene of Marcos's accident. Apparently, Marcos lost control of his truck. It did a couple of flips and landed in a ditch. Marcos had been tossed out of the truck though. He wasn't wearing his seatbelt as usual. I've always told him to put his seatbelt on. Fortunately, no one else was hurt.

Marcos was still in surgery. They explained to me with little detail that he was banged up pretty bad and to prepare for the worst. Wow. I didn't think the police would tell someone that.

I kept calm. I didn't cry because deep down inside I was hoping for the worst. I got on the phone and called Beverly, Christina his sister, Gogo his cousin, and his best friend Quan. They all met up with me within forty minutes.

After a few hours of operating a team of doctors came out to inform us that Marcos had suffered several injuries as a result of him experiencing a hemorrhagic stroke secondary to a brain aneurysm that occurred while he was driving. After further testing, they discovered that Marcos had PKD, polycystic kidney disease. I was not aware of it and wondered if Marcos was aware of it and just hadn't told me.

Well as a result of his car accident, his right leg below his knee had to be amputated. That would suck. I don't think Marcos would like that very much. He'd probably want to be dead. The doctor also explained that they would know definitely how much damage the stroke caused once Marcos awakened and they could perform further tests. One thing for sure was that he would have to undergo an intensive therapy regimen and treatment plan for both the stroke and PKD.

I was doing the happy dance in my head while the doctor was talking to me. I couldn't let everybody know I was ecstatic.

Now here I was at his bedside feeling guilty about hoping he would die. I mean I had seven kids by this man, and then there was Brittani. As bad as Marcos was, the kids still loved their father.

But I still wanted him to die.

———————

It was now the third day, and I found myself back at the hospital right at his side once again. Was I doing this because it was expected of me to show concern? Not really. Everyone knew Marcos was one of my least favorite people. To be honest, I'm not sure why I felt a need to be at his side.

Minutes passed as the machines played their usual beats creating a harmonious tune of life support. I listened and even kept up with the exhalation and inhalation of the ventilator pumping his damaged lungs with air.

I felt my face screw up with disgust as I glared down at him. I snarled in a whisper, "I hope you die."

This time he wasn't able to respond with hurtful, damaging words. He just lay there. Maybe if I accidentally trip over one of the power cords of one of these machines and pull it out of the socket...Hmmm, sounded tempting.

I said to him, "I read somewhere that one of the most painful things a comatose patient endured was the sound of a loved one's voice. They said it triggered the pain sensors of the brain and compared it to being dropped in a vat of hydrochloric acid then rolling around in salt. Now if that's the case, I guess I should get comfortable and talk to you all day."

I grunted a stifled laugh. I looked over at Marcos. Despite the accident, I could still make out that he was indeed a handsome man. Actually, he was quite pretty with pretty boy ways. I wasn't sure of how this accident was going to change his outer appearance but knowing him, it wasn't going to do anything for his inner being. Marcos was hateful and downright horrible. It would take more than an accident to change him.

"And even if you did change, I wouldn't care. You know why?" I said as if he would answer. When he didn't, I continued, "Because it's too late Marcos. I don't love you. I don't think I ever did; it was just me feeling lost and needing comfort. And what comfort you provided me! That's hilarious."

Leaning on the bedrails with my arms and hands clasped together, I let my head fall as if I was about to say a prayer. I couldn't think of anything to say. My mind went blank.

"Knock, knock, knock, knock."

Without having to look up, the soft, raspy voice was a comfort to my ears.

"Bitch, I know you ain't in here praying and crying," Corvell teased as he neared me.

I lifted my head snickering. "No. I can't believe you came up here for real."

Corvell pulled me into an affectionate embrace. "Girl, I told you I would be here for you." He cut his eyes towards Marcos. "I ain't here for his ass."

"I appreciate it," I told my childhood friend.

"So he ain't woke his yella ass up yet?"

I frowned a smile as I studied Corvell's long locs. I could have sworn he was rocking a fade last week. "What's this on your head?"

Corvell grinned and tossed his synthetic locs over his shoulders. "You like 'em girl? Lita put them in the other day. Instant locs. Baby boom!"

I laughed. Corvell was so damn animated. I examined them closer. "She got some skills 'cause she grabbed every strand of your hair up. Do they hurt?"

"No more than getting my cherry busted for the first time," he joked.

I winced. "Spare me the visual."

Corvell looked back at Marcos. "So what happens if he doesn't wake up?"

I shrugged. It was inappropriate, but I said, "I guess I'll be picking out what coffin to stuff his ass in."

Corvell narrowed his eyes at me suspiciously. "That's what you want anyway."

"For me; yes. For the kids; no."

"Well look at it this way; if he wakes up at least, you know you can outrun his ass now," Corvell laughed in reference to Marcos' amputated leg.

I punched him playfully in the arm. "Boy, stop that."

Corvell pretended as if my punch actually hurt. "Girl that hurt. You know I'm sensitive."

"That ain't what you be telling Reuben," I shot back.

Corvell scrunched his nose up in disgust. "Fuck Reuben. I got me a new man. Baby boom!"

"Do tell," I prodded.

Corvell glanced over at Marcos. "Not in front of him. I'll tell you later."

"He can't hear you."

"People in comas can hear girl!"

I laughed. My eyes landed on Marcos's and my smile instantly disappeared. The ventilator began to sound off alarming the nurse's station.

"What the fuck?" Corvell said in a panic.

That's what I thought as I stared back into Marcos' deep brown eyes. I was stuck, immobile. I know I should have rushed out of the room to flag down a nurse or a doctor, but I was shocked that he was awake. I really expected for him not to ever open his eyes again. Doom seemed to form into a gray cloud and found a spot over my head.

Would I ever rid my life of Marcos Delgado Beauchamp?

Chapter 2: *Nineteen years prior....*

My mother was Filipino. No lie she came to live in the United States because of sex trafficking. The highest bidder was a white male from America. He actually married her when she was eighteen. She gained her citizenship three years later. He ended up divorcing her once he realized she couldn't produce children and was a drug addict.

Being used for sex and using drugs most of her life had taken a toll on Lailani. Maybe it was the stress, but my mother had three failed pregnancies before I came along. She had met a black man named Benjamin Blackwood that took her in and gave her a job cleaning up office buildings. Once Ben's wife discovered he was having a little extra time with Lailani, my mother found herself out on the streets once again. However, being pregnant, she was able to obtain government assistance.

Cayce Homes was a public housing development that I would call home for years. Uneducated and very little English as a second language limited Lailani. Sometimes I think she just felt so lost that she didn't try much. The easiest thing was for her to turn to what she knew best: sex and drugs. I was left to look after my baby sister Jovelyn while my mother familiarized herself with the streets of Nashville.

Jovelyn looked at me with poverty-stricken eyes; the kinds that were sunken in due to malnutrition. She asked in her delicate voice, "Where's Mama?"

I shrugged. We hadn't seen our mama in three days, and it wasn't even the weekend yet.

"Is she bringing food for us?" Jovelyn asked.

Gunshots sounded off. It didn't sound close enough to be alarmed and worry about me and Jovelyn's safety, however, I wasn't sure of Lailani's whereabouts. She could be anywhere and bringing food home was probably the furthest thing from her mind.

I got up from our tattered couch in the living room and went to the kitchen. I knew Jovelyn was hungry. I was too, and this was why it was so important that we went to school every day. There we were guaranteed breakfast and lunch. If it wasn't for school, I don't know what we would have done as far as eating.

The cabinets were bare except for inedible items such as Crisco and baking powder. Some would probably argue that the roaches that scattered were edible. There was no point in opening the refrigerator because I knew it was empty unless a food fairy came by while we were in school.

Looking over at the clock sitting on the kitchen counter I debated on how long it would take us to walk to Corvell's and Nikki's neighborhood. Between the two of them, I'm sure I could walk away with some bread, cheese, and lunchmeat. It was five-thirty. It would be dark out by the time we made it back.

"Put on your shoes and c'mon," I told Jovelyn.

It took us forty minutes to reach Corvell's house. This wasn't my first time having to do this, so I wasn't ashamed; I was just embarrassed. And from the look on Corvell's grandmama's face, she was annoyed with me begging.

Corvell rolled his eyes and waved his grandmama off behind her back. He grinned at me though and motioned for us to come into the kitchen.

"I don't want you to get in trouble," I whispered.

"Ain't nobody thinking ''bout that old lady with her stingy ass. She don't spend none of her money for any of these groceries in here no way; my mama do," he said smacking his lips.

Corvell and I became friends because we were nerds but in a cool way. He came from a family with a little money; not much but enough to live well. His mother was a nurse and was gone most of the time. His grandmama thought she was running the house, but Corvell and his siblings weren't going for it.

Because of Corvell "sweet" ways, he was ostracized by most macho-chauvinistic males. He had such an outgoing, bubbly personality that most girls welcomed him into their circle; therefore Corvell was always amongst the popular kids just by association.

I, on the other hand, was very smart without much effort. I was a serious introvert. Most people assumed I was really shy. I was just quiet and observant. But this was my dilemma: I was poor, so I was looked down upon; however, I was known to be one of the prettiest girls in school. Being half Filipino, I possessed Asian slanted eyes. My complexion was that of caramel cream. I was petite in frame, but somehow I got the Blackwoods' females' curves. It wasn't much, but it was enough to say I had a decent shape. And what people loved the most was my hair. Unlike Jovelyn's brownish curly wavy textured hair, mine came out ink black, straight and fine. If it weren't for the way, I talked most people would assume I was one hundred percent Asian.

"Yo mama still ain't came home yet?" Corvell asked. He started packing a canvas tote from the library with various food items.

I shook my head.

Corvell plucked a box of raisin creme pies from the top of the refrigerator. He scrunched up his nose and looked over at Jovelyn. "You want these shits? I can't stand these thangs. They hers but don't say nothing."

I covered my mouth to stifle my laughter. He was giving his grandmama's raisin crème pies away without asking her first.

Jovelyn smiled and nodded. I could tell she was excited by the things Corvell was gifting us. She pointed to another box. "Can I have those too?"

Corvell frowned, "You can't have my Star Crunch. Sorry, sweetie."

"Okay," Jovelyn said defeated. Hopeful, she held up a finger. "Just one?"

Corvell gave in. He tossed a couple of the snacks into the bag.

I told him, "That's enough."

"Corvell!"

He made a face. "What Granny?"

"What?" she questioned offended.

Corvell groaned and rolled his big eyeballs. "I mean ma'am."

"Whatchu doing in there?"

"Nothing," he said. "We just talking."

"Don't be giving that girl all your mama stuff."

"Granny, she can hear you, you know that right?" Corvell asked.

"Good."

Corvell whispered, "I hate her. Nobody likes her, and that's why she at our house now."

I was used to Corvell's grandmama not taking kindly to his friends.

"Where you fixin' to go now?" Corvell asked with his hand on his hip.

"I was gonna see what Nikki was doing before we walked back home," I told him.

"Well, I'ma walk with you over there," he said.

Nikki was the third member of our close-knit friendship. She was a nerd too. As far as financial class, she fit somewhere in between Corvell and me. She lived in an apartment complex based on income. She had cousins everywhere! It seemed like she was related to everybody in the city.

Nikki was real nice. She didn't make fun of people, and she sang in the church's youth choir. She was always trying to get me to accompany her to some family function or a church event. It would be too many people for me. I attended a couple of things before, but I felt so out of place.

When we arrived at Nikki's, there was a lot of people hanging out around the breezeways and in the parking areas of the apartments. It was like this all of the time especially since it had warmed up. With only a few weeks left of school, the energy present was evident that summer was near.

"Look at y'all!"

It was Nikki's voice, but we looked around for her as we

21

approached her building. We didn't see her.

She laughed, "Right here dummies!"

We looked toward the window on the first floor at the far right of the building. Nikki was in her window grinning back at us. Instead of heading for her front door we walked over to where she was.

"What are y'all doing over here?" she asked.

"Why you talking through the window stupid?" Corvell asked. "How come you not outside like a normal person."

"I can't go outside. My mama ain't here, and I gotta watch my lil sister an'nem," she said.

"So we can't come in?" Corvell asked giving her the side eye.

"So my sister can tell my mama? No!" she said incredulously.

"Hi, Nikki!" Jovelyn grinned waving at the same time.

"Hey Jovi," Nikki responded with a smile. She looked over at Corvell and said, "You know your brother out there right?"

"Who?" Corvell asked. I could hear the aggravation already in his voice. Corvell and his brother didn't get along that good. He was close to his sister for obvious reasons.

Before Nikki could answer, Cory walked over to where we were and immediately started fucking with Corvell.

"Whatchu doing over here witcho faggot ass," Cory taunted. He tried to mush Corvell in the head, but Corvell wasn't having it.

"Go on Cory!" Corvell warned. "Don't start with me."

"Take yo ass home!" Cory growled at him. Then he had the

nerves to look at me and grin. "What's up Pretty?"

I rolled my eyes at him. I didn't like him. Cory was like every other male in our peer group who was uncomfortable with sexuality; therefore the best way for them to deal with it was by being a bully.

Now don't get me wrong; Corvell and Cory were some nice looking guys. They were tall which was why Cory was an all-star athlete. He had high college coaches coming to check him out and trying to recruit him to go to their school once he graduated.

It wasn't hard to see that the two were related. The Armstrong siblings possessed those big eyeballs that were housed in slanted heavy eyelids. They always looked like they were high or sleepy. They all were a medium pecan color. A lot of girls thought Corvell was cute but would shake their heads because he wasn't checking for them. But I will say, Corvell hadn't technically come out, but Nikki and I knew the deal.

"Oh, so you ain't gon talk to me?" Cory asked walking up on me.

"I'll talk to ya!" Jovelyn grinned. Poor child. She wanted to be everybody's friend. She was ten but had a heart of gold despite our circumstances. I didn't always feel that way, but I guess I could learn a thing or two from my younger sister.

Cory ignored Jovelyn and just kept staring at me. I didn't have any conversation for him.

"Leave her alone Cory," Corvell ordered. "Don't nobody wanna talk to your mean ass."

Cory was about to respond until someone from a white Expedition called out to him. The Expedition was nice and customized. The low volume of the bass was deep and made me wonder how profound it could get once the volume was turned up. I had seen the Expedition around before but hadn't paid much attention to it.

"C'mere lil nigga!" the driver called out.

Watching Cory jog over to the SUV, Nikki murmured, "Aw hell, he's back."

"Who is that?" I asked.

Corvell's eyes grew even bigger than what they were which I didn't think was possible. "You don't know them niggas in that truck?"

I shook my head slowly with uncertainty. "Noooo," I dragged out. "Should I know them?"

"They be over in Cayce sometimes," Corvell said.

"I mean I know I've seen the truck before, but I don't pay attention to who anybody is," I said. And I didn't. I stayed in the house and minded my business. I talked to a few of the grown folks around my building, but that was it. There were a ton of drug dealers in the projects that came and went. As long as they left Jovelyn and me alone, I didn't have to know who they were.

"So who are they? And why you say that like that Nikki?" I asked.

"Cause every time they come over here they be starting trouble," Nikki groaned.

"They run shit around here," Corvell mumbled. "And my brother stupid."

"What's he doing with them?" Nikki asked.

"Probably tryna sell drugs. And if our mama find out she

gon beat his ass," Corvell said.

"He's stoopid!" Nikki sang.

The three of us started talking about school stuff while Jovelyn just sort of twirled around in place. Poor child. I think our mama was on drugs while she was pregnant with Jovelyn.

One of our classmates, Ladonna walked over to us. She was accompanied by two other girls who I knew to be Shameka and Mia. They were in the eighth grade too, but I really didn't know them because they were in the "not so smart" classes.

"Whatchall doing over here?" Ladonna asked placing her hand on her hip. I noticed she had this weird stance like she thought she was cute. She let her legs fall back as if she was bowlegged and jutted her butt out. I mean, Ladonna was known for her big behind anyway; I wasn't sure why she felt a need to push it out even more.

"What's in the bag?" Mia asked. She was actually cute. A lot of boys thought she was pretty. She still rocked a Jerry Curl though. I think she held onto the style because her hair was down her back. She tried to convince people that it was her natural hair but you could smell *Right On* and *Carefree Curl* all over her. Besides she had like two inches of new growth that did not match the texture of her ends.

"It's our food," Jovelyn answered. I shot my sister a look.

"Food?" Shameka asked with her face frowned up. "In a library bag?"

To deter them from me, Corvell told Shameka, "You got some white shit around your mouth. Whatchu been eating or sucking on?"

"Ooh, he slick burned on you," Ladonna laughed at her

friend.

Shameka wiped at her mouth, but you could tell she was embarrassed and irritated.

"C'mon Corvell," I mumbled. "Let's go."

Before we could begin to walk away, Ladonna's older sister came walking down the sidewalk. She was wearing denim Daisy Dukes and a small halter top that showed off her small waist and flat stomach. She seemed to be putting in extra as she walked. Ladonna and her sister Ranessa had banging bodies; I'll give them that, however, they weren't the prettiest girls.

Ranessa was a senior in high school and usually being around a bunch of younger girls was not her style. But for some reason, she was joining us at Nikki's window.

In a boisterous way, she asked, "What y'all doing?" She scratched in between her box braids with one of her long colorful acrylic nails.

"Nothing," Corvell mumbled. He turned his nose up and stared at her hair and asked, "Who did your braids?"

"My sister did them," Shameka boasted. "They fye ain't they?"

Corvell side-eyed them then shot me a look. I giggled.

"Whatchu tryna say?" Ranessa asked.

"They cute," was all Corvell said. He shot me another look this time with widened eyes.

Nikki started laughing. "Corvell you're so stoopid!"

Cory walked away from the Expedition, but the driver decided to whip into one of the parking spaces right in front of where we were.

The driver, a dark-skinned guy wearing dark shades leaned out the window. "C'mere lil mama with the braids."

We all had turned in the direction of the truck; but Ranessa, the only person with braids in our group, pretended to be dumb for a second. She pointed to herself and asked with a slight smile, "Me?"

"Naw that other bitch standing beside you with braids," he said sarcastically. He chuckled, "Yeah, you!"

We watched Ranessa sashay over to the driver's side of the truck. Listening to Ranessa giggling, I understood why she came walking over to us. She simply wanted to be seen.

"Quan talking to your sister," Mia whispered to Ladonna excitedly.

The window on the passenger side slowly came down. All we saw was a toasty beige arm with corded veins resting on the door. A chunky silver Figaro link bracelet rested around the wrist. I didn't know if it was sterling silver, white gold, or platinum; it was just silver to me. The pinky ring reflected the sun's light off of it.

Then he stuck his head out. For a split second, I was drooling like the other girls, but I had to snap out of it. I didn't have time to get caught up in being boy crazy. I had other problems to worry about like keeping Jovelyn and me from starving.

"C'mere Nephia," he said.

I knew my eyes grew big. How in the hell did he know my name? We all were befuddled by that.

"Me?" I asked.

"Your name Nephia ain't it?" he asked.

I nodded. Nikki whispered, "You bet not."

"Shut up," Shameka hissed at Nikki. She nudged me forward. "You betta go on. Do you know who that is?"

I didn't, and in school, I was taught not to talk to strangers.

"C'mere," he said again. This time the tone of his voice was rather coaxing. He flashed me a smile to reassure me.

I slowly walked over still holding the library bag. When I stood by the passenger side door, I looked at him. Up close he was prettier than what I thought. And damn, he didn't even have on a shirt. He was cut up in places I didn't think was possible. The skin of both arms was riddled with tattoos. On his left wrist was a big diamond encrusted Rolex and two chains hung around his neck.

Just like Corvell he had those same sleepy/high eyes except his weren't nowhere near as big. They were slanted but had a very sultry seductive look to them. His jawline was strong, but it didn't take away from his pretty boyish look. He only wore a thin mustache, and the hair on his chin was low enough that I could make out he had one of those dimples in the center of it.

Staring at me with those deep brown eyes had me scared. It wasn't a fearful feeling, but more so nervousness. There was something very intimidating about this man's poise.

"Cory told me your name. Was that a'ight?" he asked.

I nodded. That made sense.

He looked down at my body and asked, "You go to Litton?"

I was still wearing my red, blue, and white gym uniform

from school. It had Isaac Litton Middle School all over it. I was wearing it because it was the last period I had in school that day, so I didn't bother changing just to go home.

I nodded.

"You a short lil thang. How old are you?" he asked.

"I'm fourteen," I told him. I was hoping my age would deter him from talking to me, but it didn't. I wasn't sure how old he was because of his baby face, but his body was telling me he was grown or close to it.

"What are you?"

"Huh?" I was dumbfounded.

"What are you? Your ethnicity?" he asked again.

"Oh, I'm black," I told him.

He started laughing. "No the hell you ain't. Now lie again."

I actually cracked a smile. "Okay, my mama Filipino and my daddy black."

"I knew it was some Asian shit. I can see it in your eyes," he said. His eyes lustfully scanned me from head to toe then toe to head. They rested on my hair. He asked, "All that your hair?"

I nodded. My hair was pulled up into a loose ponytail. I rarely wore it down. If I did, it was at home.

"You pretty and I think I'ma make you my wife," he told me with finality.

My eyes bucked. Then I gave him a frown grin and said, "I'm only fourteen, and I'm not looking for husbands now."

"You ain't got to 'cause I'm that nigga," he said. "Do you

29

know who I am?"

I shook my head.

"I figured you didn't," he said. He looked over at everybody at Nikki's window. "They know."

I shrugged my shoulders.

"What's that?" he asked with a frown. "You don't give a fuck about who I am?"

"I didn't say that," I responded quickly.

"Then what was that for?" he asked shrugging his shoulders imitating me.

"Nothing," I said in a low voice. I wasn't trying to upset him. I didn't know him, and I didn't know what he was capable of at that moment.

"You good though. Don't be acting all scared and shit. I ain't gon' bite you," he told me. His voice was playful. But my gut told me this bastard was sneaky. He didn't even care that I was only fourteen.

"Give me your number."

"We don't have a phone," I answered hoping that would be the end of our exchange.

"You ain't got a phone?" he asked in disbelief.

I shook my head.

"Then how will I get in touch with my future wife?"

I was flattered, but I wasn't talking to him. He must be crazy. "You probably too old for me anyway."

He started poking around in the glove compartment, but he still managed to mumble, "Age ain't nothing but a number."

"How old are you?" I was curious, so I had to ask.

"It don't even matter," he said. He handed me a red transparent pager, a black cellphone—one of the new ones with a clamshell design I might add—and the coiled charger that went to it.

"What is this for?" I asked.

"Take it. I'll hit you up okay?" he said.

"I can't—"

"Take it pretty," he told me with an infectious smile.

I was trying to figure out why my heart had started beating wildly. I was looking at him, but I wasn't understanding. I think that's when I fell under his spell. It was nothing special, but it was the way his eyes twinkled when he smiled at me in combination with the scent of his cologne that emitted from the car.

He hit Quan on the arm to get this attention. "Vamos lá!"

"A'ight," Quan said straightening up in his seat. He hollered at Ranessa as she walked away, "I'll be back through here later! Oooh got-damn! Shake that ass baby!"

"Really nigga," my guy said to Quan. He looked back at me. "See you pretty."

I was stuck. Even as the truck backed out and they took off, I was still standing there. Corvell and Shameka rushed over to me.

"He gave you that?" Shameka asked excitedly.

"Girl, you in trouble now," Corvell said shaking his head. He took the phone from me and examined it. "This nigga done gave you a damn cell phone."

"How am I in trouble? I don't even want it," I said. I tried to hand the charger and pager to Shameka. She didn't take it.

"Nuh-uh! I ain't taking it if he didn't give it to me," she said. Ladonna, Mia, and Jovelyn joined us.

Nikki hollered from the window, "I gotta go y'all! See y'all tomorrow! And Nephia…You know you done effed up right?"

I didn't know I had.

We said our goodbyes, then Corvell, me and Jovelyn headed out of the apartment complex.

"Damn, I wish you had asked him to give us a damn ride," Corvell mumbled.

"I don't want anything more from him."

"But it's too late," Corvell said.

"How? When I see him again, I'll just give it back."

"Girl, are you seriously about to reject the baddest, richest nigga around?"

"I don't care who he is."

"Let me school you," he said. "Marcos Delgado Beauchamp have ties to the Colombian cartel. His people got this city on lock. Do you understand?"

"So," I said still not getting his point.

"Whatever Marcos wants, Marcos gets. He marked you."

I found this amusing and confusing. "'Cause he gave me a damn pager and phone?"

"He just wouldn't do that to anybody Nephia."

"But why me?"

Corvell let out an aggravated groan. "Girl, have you looked in the mirror lately?"

"But I'm only fourteen. How old is this Marcos?"

"I think he's twenty-one or twenty-two," Corvell answered.

"Oh no! He's too old for me anyway."

"And you think somebody like Marcos cares?"

"He should," I said.

"Well, I'll tell you what. When he calls that phone, don't answer and see what happens."

"What's gonna happen?" I wanted to know.

"You'll see."

Chapter 3

When Jovelyn and I made it back home, our mother was there. She was sitting on the couch with a cigarette in her right hand staring back at us.

"Where you been?" she asked in her accented voice. Lailani was a very petite lady. She was very thin, the same size she was at the age of 12. At one point she was beautiful, and it was understandable why men were drawn to her exotic looks. Remnants of her beauty remained, but life and drugs had tried their best to destroy it all.

Despite the streets, Lailani was still a soft woman. I didn't always like her, but I didn't hate her; I was just disappointed in some of the choices she made. She knew it. She knew I still loved her, but the shame and guilt ate at her. It was in her eyes and in her posture.

"I had to get us something to eat," I told her. I walked into the kitchen and was stunned silent. I turned around to question her about the food on the kitchen table and counters.

She was standing there smiling displaying her discolored teeth. "I brought food. See?"

I smiled back. Jovelyn's eyes grew big with excitement. "We got more food!"

"How did you get all of this?" I asked. Lailani waved her hand dismissively. "No worry. You and Jovi put them up, please. Jovi, you take bath for school. I go to sleep."

I nodded and started putting away the groceries. Jovelyn quietly helped me. I assumed Lailani had one of her "Johns" to take her grocery shopping. There was no way she could have carried all of those bags on the bus. Maybe he gave her enough money for a cab.

Well I got my answer when Kenneth Hunter walked into the kitchen wearing a white wife beater, navy Dickies with the button undone and he was only wearing socks like he was comfortable at home.

"Daddy!" Jovelyn exclaimed wearing a grin. She could barely contain her excitement.

Kenny, on the other hand, didn't appear as excited to see his daughter. Halfheartedly he draped his arm around her as to give an unwelcoming hug as he rummaged through the refrigerator. "Hey, baby girl."

"Are you back for good Daddy?" Jovelyn asked.

I really hoped he wasn't.

Retrieving a can of beer, he answered, "Yeah, I'm back. Y'all get this stuff up 'fore it spoil."

He left out of the kitchen without even acknowledging me. I didn't like him, and even though my mama was out there in the streets while he was in prison, I still liked a life without him in it.

I tried many times over the years to let my mama know that Kenny was abusing me sexually but she either didn't get what I was saying or she was just too weak in her own shit dealing with Kenny. He used to beat her just because he felt like it. We lived in fear of him because many nights he would have us in the dark playing eenie meenie miney moe with a knife up to our throats; even to his own flesh and blood Jovelyn.

He didn't molest me like fondling here and there. He did things to me that a child shouldn't know about until they were of age. Even with my mother available, an abled-body woman with a grown woman's vagina, he would creep into the room with Jovelyn and me. She would be in her twin bed asleep, and he would get in the bed with me and do things to me until he was satisfied.

When I was younger, he would have me miss school while my mama went to work at temporary services. He would make me look at porn with him and tell me that what I was watching was what he was gonna do to me. Then he would play this game with me allowing me to get a head start to hide from him. If he found me, he would get to do those things we watched on the porn. There was never a good place to hide in our two-bedroom housing unit. I tried them all, and he would always find me. He would lay me down and remove my panties and perform oral sex on me while penetrating me with his fingers. He would then slather my opening as well as his stinky dick (it was always strong smelling) with Vaseline and try to penetrate me with it. I would cry and try to get up. He would make me be still and try again. I was too small back then. So he would just settle for sliding his dick in and out of the space where my thighs met at the junction of my vagina. He would cum and shoot the white sticky substance all over me. And it smelled too. I would feel so disgusted and dirty.

Now I didn't know if he planned to stay here or not, but I refused to stand by and let him beat on my mama again. I was older now. Watching her go through that I always vowed that I would never let a man beat on me like that. I vowed I would always protect my children if I ever had any. But I never said anything bad about him in front of Jovelyn because that was her daddy and she loved him. When she was old enough, she would see things for herself.

After making me and Jovelyn some store-bought pizza, I made her take a bath. I took mine shortly after she finished. Once I prepared myself to lay down in my twin bed across from her, I heard a ringing. It startled me at first because we didn't have a phone so I wasn't used to the noise. Then I remembered I had put the phone Marcos had given me earlier on the table next to my bed.

I looked at it and contemplated answering it. Marcos was a nobody to me. Not only was I too young for him, but I was too young to be caught up in any boys. I had plans. I was focused. I wasn't making straight A's for nothing. In the fall when I started high school, I would be in all honor classes. I already had a high school credit in Algebra that I aced with straight A's. I had dreams. I had ambition. I was going to college, and I needed a full scholarship to get there. Boys were not on my agenda.

Deciding against answering it, I placed my head on my flattened pillow and said a quick prayer to the All Mighty. Perhaps I could get Cory to give Marcos his things back.

———————

It was Thursday, and I was looking forward to Friday, so I could do absolutely nothing for the weekend. I was a loner, and I was okay with it. While everyone else would return to school on Monday talking about what went down over the weekend, I had nothing to add to it. I did a whole lot of nothing during the weekend.

"What are you over there daydreaming about?" Corvell asked me. He sat on the right of me in our last class for the day. It was Science, and nobody paid much attention to Ms.

Daniels. She was a homely white woman that wanted to be cool, but she didn't have enough bass in her voice to scare anyone. In our period, however, Corvell, Nikki and I respected her, and we tried to get everyone else to follow suit. It didn't always work though.

"Wishing it was Friday," I mumbled absently.

"Hey Nephia," Nikki said from behind us. "My mama having a card party Saturday. They gon be selling fish plates and stuff. You wanna come over?"

"I'm coming!" Corvell interjected. He turned around to face Nikki and her class partner, Montoya Gooch. "Why you ain't invited me anyway?"

"I was going to," Nikki said. She looked at me. "Are you coming?"

"Do I gotta walk over there?" I asked.

"I can get my mama boyfriend to pick you up, and we can take you back home. Oh! Why don't you just spend the night?"

That sounded tempting since Kenny was at the house now. I didn't like him being there. But what about Jovelyn?

I guess the concern was written on my face because Nikki added, "Jovelyn can come too and keep my little sister company. I'll tell my mama when I get home."

"We gotta get our steps together for the end of school rally," Corvell said.

"I got mine down," I told him. I forgot to mention that that was another reason why we were considered cool nerds. We danced on the school's half-timers team. Corvell was the captain and when I tell you he could dance his ass off; he could dance his ass off and sing!

38

I laughed and pointed behind me, "She's the one that need help."

I could feel Nikki giving me the eyes in the back of my head. "I'm not that off Nephia."

Corvell cut his eyes back at her. "We gotta work on you, honey."

"Whatever," Nikki mumbled.

Ms. Daniels walked down the aisle looking at everybody's assignments on their desk. She got to our desk and asked, "Are y'all complete with the assignment. I hear a lot of—"

Corvell held up our team assignment close to her face, "Done baby!"

"Corvell Armstrong, I am not your baby," Ms. Daniels said with a red flustered face.

Corvell smacked his lips and dug in his fresh s-curl fade, "Ms. Daniels it ain't nothing but a figure of speech, dang. If I don't call you baby who else will? You ain't got a man."

This caused a few around us that heard to snicker.

"Corvell, my personal life shouldn't concern you!" Ms. Daniels said curtly.

"It do when you ain't happy. Cause when you ain't happy, we don't get happy assignments," Corvell said.

I nudged Corvell and whispered, "Will you stop?" I looked at Ms. Daniels apologetically. "Nevermind him, Ms. Daniels. We're finished with the assignment, and we've started our homework already."

She smiled and moved on.

Yeah, Corvell could be a bit much, but I loved him

nonetheless.

The clock over the blackboard hit 3:45 p.m. and the bell rung. We jumped out of our seats gathering our belongings and tried to be the first ones to spill into the hallway. We hurried to our lockers to exchange whatever books and supplies we would need for homework. A few of us held small talk with other friends in passing but we had ten minutes to get out to our buses, or we would be left behind.

This was where I departed from Corvell and Nikki. My bus was all of the project kids. I found me a seat about midway and focused on whatever the scenery was outside that window. These kids were wild and loud. They talked about everything!

When I exited the bus to begin my journey home, I wasn't expecting to see Marcos and that white Expedition. He was with Quan, and they were talking to a group of guys right across from where the bus stopped. I pretended to not even see them and headed in the direction of my street.

Sometimes walking through the projects was like a maze to me. There were so many shortcuts to get where you were trying to go. I decided to get off the main street and cut through the yards so I wouldn't be noticed. I made it home and let myself in through the back.

Lailani greeted me with a grin. She was in the kitchen whipping up something to eat. "Hey, baby. How was school?"

"It was good," I said placing my books on the table. I headed to the freezer for a popsicle.

"You got homework?" she asked.

"I did it at school," I told her. The aroma of what she was cooking drew me closer to the stove. A smile spread across my face when I saw that she was preparing one of my favorite

Filipino dishes, chicken adobo. Next, to it, she was preparing braised collard greens. The aroma was a bit nostalgic. It reminded me of when me and Jovelyn were younger, and she loved to cook. Although the majority of our diet was American, Lailani would try to introduce us to the Philippine culture. I have learned some of the recipes, but it was a matter of having the ingredients in the house to make them.

Lailani smiled, "Jovi will be happy to see."

"Yes she will," I said. I asked, "So where is Kenny?"

"He at work," she said turning away from the stove and wiping her hands on the dish towel.

"Will he be living here again?" I asked.

She didn't want to answer me, and she avoided eye contact.

"Mama," I called out to her. She walked into the living room. I called out, "*Ina!*"

She stood by the front door peering out of the screen door and into the streets. I stood behind her. She started to speak, "I know you no like him, Nephia, but he buy food for you and Jovi. He help pay bills too."

"All he does is makes us miserable," I told her defeated. Lailani thought she was doing what was best for her daughters, but she was sadly mistaken. How could I get through to her?

"But I'm not misery! Jovi is not misery," she told me.

I just said the word the right way, but she still didn't say it that way. I always thought that was funny whenever she did that.

"Where is Jovi?" she asked.

41

I looked outside and saw that the other elementary school kids were walking to their homes, but there was no Jovelyn. A frown covered my face. "I don't know. She should be walking with Domonique."

I stepped out on the front porch and called out to Jovelyn's friends. "Hey, Domonique! Where is Jovi?"

"She still at the bus stop with Quanisha an'nem!" Domonique answered.

"Okay," I told her. I turned back to Lailani, "I'll go get her."

Lailani nodded.

The bus stop where the elementary kids got dropped off was just a street over from our building. As I walked down the sidewalk I spotted the white SUV on the opposite side of the street, but it was a ways down; however, it was directly across from where the bus stop was. And I didn't see Jovelyn.

Cautiously, I slowed down and looked around. There was music coming from the SUV, but it wasn't loud enough that I couldn't hear children's laughter coming from the other side of it. If Jovelyn was over there, I was gonna slap her silly. She knew better, and she knew she was supposed to bring her tale directly home!

God, I didn't want to go over there to see if she was there. I crossed the street and walked in between the parked cars on the curb. Keeping my distance, I looked down the walk, and there she was with a group of kids beside the SUV.

And so was *he*.

There he was in a white tank with white baggy pants that rested on his hips displaying his white boxers. On his feet were wheat, Timbs. It seemed as if he was blinging more this day than he was the day before. His exposed golden muscular arms were looking mighty nice though.

"Jovi!" I called out.

She looked up in my direction and grinned and waved. I heard her say, "There's my sister!"

God, Jovelyn was so slow!

Marcos and his crew all looked down in my direction. Marcos didn't look too pleased.

Ignoring him and staying right where I was, I called out to her, "C'mon! You're supposed to be at home!"

When she started to sprint towards me, Marcos grabbed her. He said something to her, and she nodded with a grin. She didn't move. It angered me, and the vexation showed on my face.

Holding onto Jovelyn, Marcos called out, "Come get her."

Jovelyn thought this was a game because I could see her giggling. It was his way of getting me to come be in close range of him. But I had to get my sister.

I inhaled and prepared myself for whatever games Marcos was about to play.

When I got close enough, I reached out for Jovelyn. "Mama's worried about you."

Instead of Jovelyn taking my hand, Marcos grabbed it and literally yanked me to him and dragged me around to the back of the truck.

"What the fuck up with you?" he asked. His brows furrowed into a scowl as he looked down at me.

Marcos wasn't as tall as I thought he was from seeing him yesterday. Of course, he was taller than my petite five feet and two inches frame. In the clutches of his arms, he had me on my tip toes. I didn't know whether to think he was a lunatic or if I should really be fearful of my life. Later I would learn that I should have thought both.

My mouth opened to say something, but my voice was caught in my throat. Did he realize he had me almost off the ground?

I guess he saw the terrorized look in my eyes and he let me down. Angrily he asked, "Why didn't you answer the phone when I called last night?"

"I went to bed early," I lied.

"You went to bed early," he repeated as if he was trying to comprehend what I had said. "From now on don't go to bed until I call you."

I nodded my understanding.

His face finally creased into the charming smile he flashed me the day before. "I didn't mean to come on so rough like that. You too pretty for a nigga to be roughing you up, but I will if I have to."

Okay, I thought maybe he was looney. I should have taken heed to his words. He let me know right then that he had no qualms about putting his hands on women.

"I gotta get my sister back home," I told him.

"That's cool. Your sister is a trip. I didn't realize you lived over here until I saw her. I thought you lived where I saw you yesterday."

"That's where my friends live. I was just visiting."

Sensing my nervous energy, he asked, "Are you scared of me?"

Was that what I was feeling? Fear? My answer came out small and hoarse, "A little."

He chuckled and gave me a reassuring smile, "You don't have to be. I want you to be mine one day."

"I don't even know you."

"You can get to know me. But first, you need to learn how to answer that goddamn phone I gave you," he said in a playful angered tone.

I smiled nervously. "Okay." The smile disappeared, and I had to ask one more time. "You know I'm only fourteen right? I'm still in the eighth grade."

"Don't worry 'bout all that," he said looking down at his buzzing pager. He looked back at me. "You got the looks I want in the woman I make my wife. I ain't never laid eyes on a female as pretty as you. All exotic and shit."

"So you're gonna wait until I turn eighteen?"

"Wait for what?" he asked as if he was clueless.

"I mean, aren't you...grown?"

Again he said, "Don't worry 'bout all that. I wanna take you out this weekend. Take you shopping. A pretty girl like you need to be in only the best. And if you act right, I'll take you out of these bricks real soon."

What was that supposed to mean?

"Go on and take your lil sister home. I'll be calling you tonight."

I turned to walk away, but he stopped me. He pulled me

into his arms and hugged me ever so gently. It felt good, and he smelled magical!

He sent me off with a slap to my ass. For some reason, it didn't offend me. I looked back at him and gave him a frowning smile.

"C'mon Jovi," I said grabbing her by the arm and pulling her along. Her friends yelled out their goodbyes. Marcos' crew gave me these teasing grins as I walked past them. And I got this eerie feeling I was being watched. I looked around and some of the girls I went to school with along with some of the older women were looking at me. I couldn't tell what exactly was coming off from them because some wore disgusted looks, others wore looks of awe and surprise, and others wore looks of jealousy.

Later I would learn that what I sensed was correct. Most young adult women wanted the attention I was getting from Marcos. Why? Because he had money? No one seemed to care that he was crazy.

———————

Later that night, I actually felt myself growing anxious waiting for that phone to ring. Maybe he would forget and not call me at all. I was feeling rather disappointed if he didn't call me. But I didn't understand where these feelings were all coming from.

It was almost ten when the phone rang. I quickly answered it so that it wouldn't wake Jovelyn or alarm Lailani and Kenny in the other room.

"Hello?" I whispered.

"What's up?"

"Nothing," I meekly said. I was wearing this stupid grin that I hope he couldn't detect over the phone.

"You betta had answered this phone this time," he said.

"Or what?"

He chuckled in disbelief. "Or what? You got a little sass to you don't you?"

I giggled. "Not really."

"I believe you do. You tryna come off all innocent and shit. Keep reminding me you only fourteen. You don't carry yourself like you're only fourteen."

"Well, I am. And isn't it illegal for a man your age Marcos to be talking to someone my age?"

"First of all, fuck the law. Secondly, I see you know my name now. You know how old I am too?"

"I knew your name yesterday. And you're twenty-one. That's a whole seven years older than me."

"Actually I'll be twenty-two in November but like I said, fuck that. Who telling any damn way?"

"I don't know."

"Exactly. Don't worry 'bout that shit. What I want you to focus on is being ready Saturday when I come to pick you up."

"You're serious huh?"

"That's one thing I don't do; I don't play. And I need you to get with the program. I ain't used to all this resistance. I understand this might be new to you but when I saw you yesterday...I don't know. You caught my attention and interest. Answer this question for me and answer it honestly? Are you fucking?"

I was stunned silent.

"It's a simple question. Are you fucking or have you fucked?"

Did Kenny count? I didn't know how to answer the question. I wanted to say I was still a virgin being that Kenny never penetrated me with his man part; however, I'm sure my hymen was no longer intact due to Kenny's rough finger fucking. But was this really Marcos's business?

"Why?" I asked.

"Don't worry 'bout it. I'll find out," he said. "If you got some little boys sniffing after you, tell them you belong to Marcos now."

I was getting nervous again. It slipped my mind that Nikki wanted me to come over Saturday. "I forgot. I gotta go somewhere Saturday."

"Cancel it. I'll be at your house Saturday around three. You gon' be with me all day."

"But I ain't really got anything cute to wear," I told him.

"Don't even worry 'bout that either," he said. "Nephia, I'm 'bout to expose you to a way better life than you used to over in them bricks sweetness."

I smiled, "Okay."

I could hear the smile in his voice too. "I figured you'd see it my way. I'ma let you get some sleep. What time you get out of school?"

"Three forty-five," I told him.

"A'ight," he said. "Go to sleep baby and dream about me."

I smiled even bigger. "Okay."

"Bye love."

He hung up, and I just held the phone. What was I getting myself into?

Chapter 4

Nikki and Corvell looked at me like I was crazy. We were on lunch break in the cafeteria at our usual table. I had just told them about my conversation with Marcos the night before.

"So you ain't coming to my house Saturday?" Nikki asked.

"I will have him drop me off there later," I told her.

"I'm mad 'cause I wanna go," Corvell pouted.

"Well forget you too Corvell," Nikki said playfully. She looked back to me. "I think you're making a mistake messing with this dude."

"I'm not gonna mess with him like that," I tried to assure them. They weren't falling for it.

"Didn't you say he asked you if you were fucking?" Corvell asked.

"Who are y'all talking about?" Montoya asked.

Corvell quickly replied, "Mind your business."

"Well y'all talking around me. We wanna know what y'all talking about too," Montoya said looking at her friend Turkessa.

"You know Marcos?" Nikki asked.

Turkessa's mouth dropped open. "Marcos like drug dealer Marcos?"

"Yeah him," Nikki said.

Corvell corrected, "Well technically Marcos isn't a drug dealer. He has connections with people that are."

"It's all the same. His hands get dirty too," Nikki waved off.

"I heard they were clean," Corvell argued. "Why hadn't the feds been able to lock his ass up?"

"The McQuiddies are still running around here free too," Montoya mentioned.

"Uhm...Marcos Delgado and the McQuiddies are on two different levels," Turkessa said. "Meaning Marcos got more paper that can do more talking for him than the McQuiddies."

"Regardless, he's trouble," Nikki said. She pointed to me and said, "And this crazy girl been talking to him."

"Talking to him? Like talking to him?" Turkessa asked with surprise.

"Why is that so shocking?" I asked.

"Oh, it ain't. You're his type anyway. I'm just shocked to know somebody he trying to holla at. You betta get with him," Turkessa said.

"He's too old for her," Nikki pointed out.

"So. When she's twenty-six, he'll be what? Thirty-three or something like that. Will it matter then?" Montoya interjected.

"That's then. She'll be of consenting age," Nikki countered.

"Are you jealous?" Turkessa teased. Leave it to Turkessa to stir the pot.

"No, I'm not jealous," Nikki insisted. She looked at me with genuine concern in her eyes. "I just want Nephia to be careful. I heard he wasn't that nice to women."

I thought he couldn't be worse than Kenny. But why was I giving Marcos any thought anyway? Was it the idea of being taken out of the bricks and being bought new things getting to me? It did sound appealing.

"I'll be careful. We're just talking right now anyway. No harm will be done until he crosses that line; a line I'm not trying to cross any time soon," I told them. Did I convince them? Because I sure didn't feel convinced.

The remainder of the school day, my mind kept drifting to thoughts of Marcos. This wasn't supposed to be happening to me. I was supposed to be focused. It was why I never wanted to get caught up in being boy crazed. But Marcos was different from all the other little boys that tried to talk to me.

The last bell rung, and I flew out of gym. I congregated in the lobby of the school by the lockers to exchange my goodbyes with my friends. Suddenly we heard the loud bass of someone's car audio system. It was playing a Tupac track from his *All Eyez on Me* album. I wasn't a real big Tupac or hip-hop fan, so it didn't get me hyped like everyone else. Then another audio system came bumping even louder music. Some people even rushed to see who was out there.

I looked back at Corvell and Nikki, "I gotta go before the bus get all crowded, and I got nowhere to sit."

"Okay! Call me and let me know," Nikki said.

"Call you?" I asked. "On what?"

"Your cell phone!" Nikki and Corvell both hollered out.

I totally forgot. "Oh yeah!"

I hurried through the cluster of students and ran outside.

"Nephia!"

I heard my name being called, but I wasn't sure. I looked from side to side and even back thinking it was Corvell. It wasn't, so I proceeded to my bus. As usual, I found me a midway seat and focused on the scenery outside the window.

A girl I knew to be in the seventh grade came on the bus and said, "Nephia, that guy out there want you."

Was she talking to me?

She looked out of the window on my side and pointed. "Right there."

This other hot ass girl I knew from the other team of eighth graders opposite of our eighth-grade wing, said, "Ooh! You know Marcos an'nem?"

That's when I looked out the window and saw the white SUV and of course Marcos in his all-white attire. I was beginning to believe that was the only color he wore.

A smile spread across my face. I let my window down and hollered out, "What?"

"What?" Marcos echoed as he stepped closer to the bus. "Getcho ass off this damn bus and c'mon!"

He didn't have to tell me twice. I gathered my things and hurried off the bus.

"Where you going?" asked Corvell who had finally made it outside.

"Marcos is over there," I smiled.

Corvell grinned too. "Look atchu! Well, go head witcho bad self!"

"I'll call you," I said and ran in between the row of buses to get to Marcos. And in front of all of my schoolmates, he gave me the biggest hug. I was feeling special now.

"Get in this truck girl," he told me. He opened the door to

the back for me to get in. He got in right behind me.

I was instantly impressed with the inside of the SUV. I hadn't been inside anything that was this nice. Everything was customized with his initials MDB. It was strange because I had never seen Marcos driving this vehicle. And today Quan wasn't in the driver's seat. It was another guy.

"A'ight lil nigga! Tell yo brotha holla at a nigga or somethin," the driver was telling some boys outside his window. He looked back at me and Marcos. He smiled at me. "What's up Lil Mama?"

"Hi," I said coyly.

"Nigga, don't talk to my girl," Marcos said with a joking smile. He ordered, "Drive to Green Hills."

A girl sat in the passenger seat. She looked back at me and gave me a half smile. She was pretty, but she looked just as young as I did. And there was something about that half smile that gave me pause. She seemed upset about something.

"Nephia, that nigga driving is Gogo, my stupid ass cousin," Marcos told me. Looking at Gogo, I could see the family resemblance. He too looked like he could be mixed with whatever Marcos was mixed with. Gogo had really long cornrows that flowed down his back, and he appeared taller and slimmer than Marcos.

Marcos continued, "And that's his girl, Bridgette."

She turned back to me and spoke softly, "Hi."

"Hey," I said. I think she had been crying or something. I wanted to know what was wrong with her.

"Where your phone and pager?" Marcos asked me.

"At home," I answered.

"What's the point of having them if you gonna keep that shit at home?"

I shrugged. "I didn't want to bring it to school with me, and someone steal it."

"Once they realize whose girl you are they won't try to steal shit from you."

"Who are you? I mean why should everyone be so fearful of you?" I asked.

I wanted to take the question back after the way he looked at me.

"*Usted pronto descubrirá,*" was all he said. I didn't speak a lick of Spanish, so I just stared at him. Later I would learn that he basically said I will soon discover; however, by the time I knew what he said, it was too late.

During the ride to the Green Hills area, he tried to get me to relax. He even put his arm around me and pulled me close to him. He was making me nervous especially when I could feel his lips brushing against my neck. It instantly made me hot, but I was scared. This was completely different than what Kenny took me through. I could feel reciprocated desires for Marcos.

"You don't kiss?" he whispered in my ear.

I shook my head.

"You're about to now," he said.

The softness of his voice made me putty in his hands. I allowed him to kiss me. I didn't know what I was doing. I even giggled in his mouth as he tried to part my lips to ease his tongue inside. He called me silly, but it didn't stop him. I continued until I got control of my giggles and actually returned the kiss back. It wasn't so bad. It actually felt good and stirred something in the pit of my stomach. I don't know what it was, but it caused me to ache.

He pulled back and smiled at me, his eyes twinkled, and I was his again. "Now that wasn't that bad."

"It wasn't," I agreed.

"Have you ever been kissed down there?"

"Down where?" I asked stupidly. Of course, I knew what he was talking about.

To make sure I knew what he was talking about he slid his hand in between my legs and rubbed me there causing me to throb and jump. My breathing almost stopped.

"What's it doing so hot in between there?" he asked.

"I don't know," I whispered.

He gave me a doubting side eye look. Then he looked down at his crotch. I could see it poking through his pants. What the hell?

"See what you're doing to me?" he asked.

I giggled. "Make it go down! That's nasty!"

He laughed uncontrollably at me. "You so damn young!"

What was I thinking! What had I done? I allowed this man to mesmerize me and I got completely off focused. I totally forgot about being home for Jovelyn. What if Lailani wasn't there when she got home from school? I hope that girl had enough sense to go next door to Ms. Cheryl's house. But shame on me for forgetting about my sister.

I was a mess by the time I realized my mistake. Marcos

tried his best to keep me calm. He had no problem with getting me back home as soon as possible. I had such a good time that I hated to end the day with him though. I had all kind of shopping bags in my hands. And all of it wasn't for just me. I got Jovelyn some things as well as a couple of new things for Lailani. I even picked up a couple of shirts for Corvell and got Nikki some expensive lip gloss. I don't know exactly how much Marcos spent on me because I stopped hanging around for the total after the first two stores. He had no problem at all with pulling out wads of cash to pay for everything.

Before I could hop out of the SUV, he pulled me back. "Wait a minute. Hold up. Don't I get a kiss?"

I leaned over and this time without hesitation I kissed him softly on the lips. I pulled back to smile at him. "Thank you, and I'll see you tomorrow."

"That's exactly what I wanted to hear. I'll call you later."

I hurried out of the car and headed down the walk to my door. The main door was opened, so someone was home. Thank goodness!

I struggled while trying to get in the house with all of the shopping bags.

"Nephia!" Jovelyn jumped up from the floor. "Where have you been?"

Lailani came around the corner from the kitchen. She looked angry at first, but when she saw everything in my hands, she softened. She asked anyway, "Where were you?"

"I'm so sorry!" I said apologetically.

"What's all that Nephia?" Jovelyn asked pointing to the bags.

I grinned and searched for the things I got her. I pulled out several articles of clothing for her. Her eyes grew big.

"Are these for me? They're mine?" Jovelyn asked excitedly.

"Yes!" I told her.

Lailani smiled. "Where you get this from?"

Kenny started coming down the stairs.

"I got something for you too Mama," I told her. I started digging around for the dress I picked out for her. I also got her matching sandals.

Her eyes told me she loved it. As soon as she reached out for it, Kenny stepped in and snatched it away. "You don't need this shit!"

I looked at him in disbelief. "What are you doing?"

"She ain't taking this shit. Neither is Jovi. Put that shit down!" he barked.

Jovelyn looked as though she would cry. It had been a long time since any of us had anything new to wear.

"Why?" Lailani wanted to know.

Kenny turned to me and demanded to know, "Did you steal this?"

"No!" I said in a more defensive tone than I intended.

"Who the fuck was that you just got out the car with?" he asked.

"A friend!" I shouted.

"Who the fuck you shouting at?"

Lailani stepped in between us. "No, no. No yelling and fighting."

"A friend got this for me," I said in a calmer tone.

"Give it back!" Kenny ordered.

"Why Daddy?" Jovelyn asked through tears.

He turned to Lailani. "I just seen her out the window kissing some boy. You got her turning tricks now?"

"No!" Lailani answered adamantly. "Never. Nephia, how you get this?"

"I told you, my friend," I told her. I could feel myself on the verge of tears.

"You have sex for these?" Lailani asked. Disappointment clouded her face.

I shook my head. "No, *Ina*."

"And you don't think that's what he's expecting in return?" Kenny countered.

I wanted to ask him what was *he* expecting in return, but I said nothing. I looked at my mama desperately to see what she wanted me to do.

"Take things to your room. I'll be there to talk with you," Lailani said.

I looked at Jovelyn and asked, "Can you help me get these upstairs."

Sniffling she eagerly obliged.

I didn't bother with putting the things away until I was sure my mama would be okay with it. It didn't stop Jovelyn from modeling her things though. She was really happy with what I got her. I didn't want to have to take them back from her.

———————

Lailani talked with me after we ate dinner. I insisted that I wasn't having sex. She asked me if I intended on having sex soon. I thought that was odd. I told her I didn't have intentions of having sex yet. She asked me who the friend that I was with earlier. I told her he wasn't a boyfriend; just a friend that wanted me to have nice things. Just as Kenny tried to say downstairs, she also told me that guys didn't just do things like that for no reason. He would want something in return. Deep down inside I knew that was the case. I was hoping Marcos would be understanding and not pressure me.

Lailani told me we could keep the things. She told me to hold onto her gifts. She didn't want Kenny upset. I understood. I hated that I lied to her though. I told her that Jovelyn and I were spending the night at Nikki's for the weekend and that we would be back Sunday. She was okay with that. In actuality, Marcos was coming to get me and Jovelyn and dropping her off at Nikki's while I went on with him. I called Nikki, and she was willing to cover for me...reluctantly.

I confirmed all of this by phone that night with everyone.

I don't know what time it was when Kenny decided to join me in my bed that night. I know Jovelyn was knocked out. He startled me, and I almost screamed when I awakened to find him in my bed. He had covered my mouth and put his finger up to his lip to quiet me.

When he was sure, I was fully awake and wouldn't scream he removed his hand.

"So you giving pussy away?" he whispered.

I shook my head. I felt his hands tugging at my panties. I placed my hands over his to stop him. "What are you doing?"

"If anybody gonna get this it's gonna be me."

"No!" I whispered yelled.

"Shut the fuck up!" he warned. "Now move your goddamn hands."

"I will scream," I threatened.

"You do, and I'll kill everybody in here."

I believed him.

I blurted out, "I'm on my period!"

"I don't believe you."

"Please don't," I begged.

He tugged my panties down leaving me open and exposed. He crawled on top of me and slid down until his head was in between my legs. I closed my eyes tight and caught my breath as soon as I felt his cold tongue invade my slit. His finger started probing until it found my opening. He licked on me and fingered me until he felt I was ready. Raising to his knees, he pushed his pajama pants down exposing his hard erection. Spreading my legs apart, he held himself as he guided it towards my opening. When I felt his head prying at my opening, I started to silently cry.

"Daddy?" Jovelyn's voice was raspy as she tried to focus on what she was seeing.

Hearing her jolted him from his plan of actions. He quickly raised his pants back up and hopped out of my bed. "What is it, baby?"

"Why are you in our room? What's wrong with Nephia?" Jovelyn asked.

Thank you baby sis!

"She was having a nightmare. I was just making sure she was okay," he lied. "Go back to sleep baby. Everything is alright. She's okay."

Jovelyn sat up and looked over at me. Even in the darkness, she could sense that I wasn't okay. "Well, I'm gonna sleep over there with her to make sure she's okay."

"That's a good idea," he said.

As Jovelyn made her way to my bed, I quickly pulled my nightshirt down because I had no idea where my panties were. I moved over to make room for her. She got in the bed and wrapped her arms around me tight. She whispered, "I won't let the boogeyman get you."

Chapter 5

Saturday had come, and I was truly welcoming of the change. I was glad to be doing something different and around different people although most everyone was older than me. I learned that Bridgette was actually sixteen and Gogo was nineteen. That wasn't too bad of an age difference. She was the only one closest in age to me. She and I hit it off well. The older ladies, a white girl named Carrie and some other mixed looking girl named Jessica didn't take to us that well.

Carrie was there as Quan's date, and Jessica was Boogie's date. Boogie was another friend of Marcos's. Without much asking, I learned that Boogie, Quan, and Gogo were Marcos's "yes men." They catered to Marcos's every need without question. I also learned that Quan and Boogie were big-time street drug dealers. I wasn't really comfortable with that, but Marcos assured me that this outing was strictly for fun and relaxing.

I was still curious about what Marcos did that he could carry around large wads of money and have other guys to bow down to him.

As we were leaving the movies, he grabbed me under his arms. "Did I tell you, you're looking good today?"

I blushed. "I think you did already."

"Are you sure you're only fourteen?" he asked again.

I nodded. I did feel kind of grown and sexy in the long fitting wraparound brown checkered skirt I was wearing designed by Christian Dior. I matched it with a bronze silk collared crop blouse that displayed my waist and stomach. I wore chunky high heeled strappy sandals that I got from Gucci. I had never worn anything designer in my life. It felt really good. To top it off you couldn't tell me nothing with the brown Gucci bag I was carrying. I had my hair twisted up and held by a claw clip in the back allowing the rest to cascade over messy-like albeit flirty. I smelled lovely with a fruity Victoria Secret's cucumber melon body spray and lotion, and my lips were kissed perfectly with a hint of Bobbi Brown lip gloss.

I found myself enamored by Marcos by the time we made it to dinner. I felt good around him. He constantly told me how pretty I was. He couldn't resist touching me either. Unlike Kenny, Marcos's attention seemed affectionate. He made me giddy and gave me butterflies. Besides, he was a lot better to look at than Kenny.

We went to this place called Delgado's. It was a classic American restaurant with South American specialty dishes thrown in the mix like fried plantains or Pantacones as Marcos pronounced for me. I ate Filipino dishes, so trying South American dishes wasn't going to be a terrible feat for me. So I ordered from the South American menu. I think it impressed Marcos. After I told him how good the dishes were, he told me that the restaurant was owned by his family. It was actually Gogo's family running the place. His father Carlos was the head chef. The place was really nice, and no expense was spared making it the wonderful atmosphere that it was. The perks of eating at the family restaurant of course were I could get whatever I wanted, and Marcos slipped me a frozen margarita. And I must say it had me right!

I was feeling good and a little tipsy by the time we left. Marcos pulled me back to the third-row seating of the Expedition on our way home. He wasted no time devouring me in aggressive kisses and touching me in places that had me nervous but had me hot at the same time. My young loins were screaming for more.

Before I knew it, he had my one leg thrown over his lap while his hand eased up under my skirt as he sucked on my neck and lips. I didn't bother to stop him. He went on to hook his finger around my panties and slipped his finger inside me. He fingered me and kissed me wildly as I lost myself in the moment. He grabbed my hand and placed it on his hardness. I wasn't sure of what I was supposed to do so I started rubbing it. He dug deeper inside me then pulled out just enough to rub my clitoris. What the hell he do that for? I grabbed his hand because it was too much to bear.

"Stop," he whispered to me. I wouldn't let his hand go. He bit me gently on my neck until I loosened my hold on his hand. He consoled me. "Just relax. I promise I just wanna make you feel good."

That's what I was afraid of. I wasn't sure if my young mind was ready for this. Have I mentioned that I was only fourteen?

Marcos removed his hand from under my skirt and looked to Boogie who was driving. "*Llévame hombre casa. Tengo que cuidar mi amor derecha.*"

"English nigga!" Boogie said looking in the rearview mirror at Marcos's reflection.

Gogo laughed. "Take the nigga home!"

Boogie asked in a serious tone, "Home nigga?"

Marcos nodded. "*Mi casa!*"

"You sure?" Boogie asked once more for certainty.

"Yes!"

I wanted to know why that was such a big deal.

Boogie asked, "To the big house?"

Marcos nodded. *"Estoy a punto de coger a esta joven coño!"*

Gogo laughed. I really needed to learn Spanish.

Marcos chuckled with a devious smirk. He looked at me and told me, "You're coming home with me tonight."

I opened my mouth to object, "But I gotta get back to Nikki's."

"They'll be alright without you. They won't even miss you," he said.

"I've never spent the night with a boy," I said.

"I ain't a boy," he said, grabbing his erection for emphasis.

I wasn't sure about any of this.

Marcos caressed my face softly in a loving way. "You'll be okay baby. I won't hurt you. I promise."

I simply nodded. I let him kiss me again. For the rest of the way to his place, I just sat close to him, nuzzled into his chest. We didn't say much. He talked on his cell phone in Spanish for a little bit. I had to learn Spanish.

When Boogie pulled up to a gated property, I was a little thrown. I couldn't see the actual house, but I assumed it was Marcos's *casa*. Boogie punched in a code on the keypad at the gate, and it opened allowing us access.

The driveway circled up to a Spanish style mansion with a front courtyard. I could see that there were three separate garages facing the front. Since it was night, lights shown on the property from the ground. The inside was lit as well. There was a big lighted fountain in the middle of the courtyard that was too astounding for words.

I didn't have any questions. I just let Marcos escort me out of the car. He said a few words to Boogie and Gogo before he pulled me along to the front entrance of this magnificent house.

Once inside, just standing in the foyer, I could take in the beauty of the home. I still didn't ask any questions. A middle-aged black maid in uniform approached us. "Is there anything I can get you and your guest, Mr. Beauchamp?"

"Not right now Ada," he said. He looked back at me and reached out for my hand. "C'mon my sweet."

As he led me down corridor after corridor, we finally made it to the west wing of the house where his bedroom was. I realized as I took in the décor along the way that Marcos had a thing for the color white. This house was white everywhere. His bedroom was like a magical winter land of ice crystals and snow.

"You can get comfortable," he told me. He disappeared into what I assumed was a huge walk-in closet.

I made my way over to his huge bed and sat down. In my brown clothing, I felt so out of place in the sea of white. I looked around and noticed he had his own private bar in his bedroom. There was a nice stereo system embedded in the wall. I didn't see a television anywhere and assumed he didn't have one in the bedroom.

Marcos came back out of the closet in only a pair of white boxer briefs. All of his jewelry was gone except for the princess cut diamond earrings in his ears and the white gold chain with the diamond cross pendant around his neck.

I wasn't sure if he worked out regularly, but his body

couldn't be the way it was by genetics only. Even his legs were powerfully muscular. And I couldn't tear my eyes away from his print poking out at his boxer briefs.

"I told you to get comfortable," he told me. He knelt down before me and began removing my sandals. "Do I gotta do it for you?"

I didn't say anything. I just watched him do it.

"I know you got a ton of questions for me," he said as he remained focused on undressing me.

"You'll tell me whatever you want me to know," I said.

"In due time, I'll tell you everything. I just gotta make sure you're the one," he said. He began unbuttoning my crop top.

"The one for what?" I asked.

"The one to share my life with."

"Don't you think I'm too young? I got four more years of school before I'm even grown."

"I wish you quit saying that," he said. He moved in close to me to reach behind me and unfasten my bra.

"You don't even know me, Marcos," I pointed out.

"I will," he said. He stared at my breasts. It was then I realized I was bare-chested in front of him. It was too late to cover up, but I wanted to so bad.

Let me roll with this. I leaned back on my arms and gave him a look enticing him to continue.

He licked his lips and gave me this wicked smile. He tugged at my skirt's ties to loosen it up so it would easily slip off. Eventually, I was before him in only my white bikini panties.

As if I was some exquisite piece of art he roamed his hands over my body gently, carefully. He massaged my handful of breasts before taking them in his mouth. This sensation was new to me; the feel of a man's mouth on my nipples. I could tell he was enjoying this as much as it was making me feel. He started to get more aggressive causing my nipples to ache. I groaned.

"I want you bad," he whispered to me. He kissed me softly on my lips. "But you're not ready are you?"

I bit my bottom lip in between my teeth. "I don't know."

"You're not a virgin are you?" he asked.

"Why you ask me that?"

"There was no blood. Your cherry's been busted already. Either you've fucked before or you been letting some nigga play in this pussy for a minute," he said.

"I've done stuff," was all I said.

"So does that mean you've had dick penetration?"

I shook my head.

A sly smile covered his face. "Can I be the first?"

I smiled a little but gave an uncertain shrug.

"Tonight?" he asked.

"I don't know," I said coyly.

He stood to his full height before me and pulled down his boxer briefs without hesitation. His dick stuck straight out at me. There was a clear liquid at the tip like a drop of dew.

I was fascinated. Without thinking, I reached out and touched the clear substance with my finger. "What is this?"

"That's pre-cum. It means I wanna fuck the shit out of you."

I looked up at him to see how serious he was. He was serious. Still fascinated I wrapped my hand around him. It was hot and felt like it was pulsating in my hand. It was definitely thick. The head was just as girthy as the shaft. It looked like some of the other dicks I had seen on the porns I watched with Kenny. It was bigger than Kenny's too. I wasn't sure if I was ready for it, but it seemed as though he was growing harder and thicker the more I held onto him.

I released him.

"Do you want to proceed?" he asked me.

The seriousness in his tone let me know this was no longer a game for him. Either I wimped out like the fourteen-year-old girl I was, or I acted the age he needed me to be. A thought flashed through my mind thinking about I could be at home getting misused and abused by Kenny against my will.

I nodded.

Wasting no more time, he eased out of his briefs and climbed on top of me. He kissed me then whispered, "I've been waiting for this all night."

He kissed me again this time parting my lips using his tongue to caress mine. I went along with it returning the kiss imitating whatever he did. My hands began to wander and touched him everywhere. I loved the feel of his rippled muscles. He kissed down my neck and over my collarbone. Eventually, his mouth found its way to my breasts again. He closed his lips around my nipples encircling them with his tongue causing them to harden and ache even more. A moan sounded from me. He found his way back up my neck and to my lips again where we locked in a sensual, aggressive kiss.

I could feel him grinding his thickness into my panty covered pie. He wanted in bad, but for some reason, he wasn't rushing. He had me hot, and I was ready.

He pulled away from my lips long enough to ask me tenderly, "Can I taste you?"

I nodded again.

Keeping our bodies still touching in some way Marcos eased down in between my legs. He kissed down my thighs before sliding my panties off. He positioned himself back in between my legs right in front of my love box. He held my legs open and eased one of his fingers inside me. Slowly he picked up a nice rhythm while locking his gaze on mine.

"You like how this feel Nephia?" he asked me.

I did, and it was weird because it was what Kenny did to me all the time, but it felt nothing like how Marcos was making me feel.

He continued to talk soothingly to me as he finger-fucked me. "You got some tight wet pussy and you ready for this dick too."

My hips began rocking on their own against the thrust of his finger. He eased another one inside me preparing me for the thickness of him. I closed my eyes enjoying the slow rhythm of his fingers going in and out caressing my walls and stimulating my juices to flow. His thumb gently worked its magic on my clit in a circular motion. I whimpered and tremored in response to his touch. He kissed my knee and planted kisses down my inner thighs from one to the next. He removed his fingers to spread my pussy lips apart. He then explored every fold and surface of my pussy with his tongue causing me to cry out in pleasure. It seemed as if his mouth covered me in a French kiss. When his lips closed around my clit and suckled it ever so gently I didn't know what to do. I grabbed his head and moaned, "Marcos!"

He continued to tickle my clit until I couldn't take any more. It seemed like the more he did it, the more ticklish it became, and I felt like exploding with laughter. That explosive laughter I thought was building up inside me was actually me on the brink of having an orgasm. And because Marcos refused to stop it took me to the edge once again. But instead of laughter, a much more intense sensation took over my body; something I couldn't quite explain because it captured me by surprise. It was a scary feeling, but at the same time, it was a joyous one too. Nonetheless, it was overwhelming. The laughter turned into a loud wailing scream that I couldn't control. It just came out. My body tensed, and I could feel my pussy walls contracting rapidly.

Definitely caught off guard, I became somewhat apprehensive and frightened. Marcos could sense it. He was so caring and loving about it. He came up to hold me and place delicate kisses on my face to vanquish the worry. "Are you okay? Do you want to continue?"

I nodded.

He didn't rush, but he continued to kiss on my body here and there. I could feel the warmth and hardness of him against me. He was still ready as ever. When he returned to my face, he started kissing me passionately on the lips. Our tongues wrestled with one another as he slowly began grinding into me again. He intertwined my hands with his, and for some reason, I felt a connection with him. I felt closer to him. I was completely comfortable with him.

As we continued to kiss and grope at one another somehow, he worked himself deeper in between my legs. My legs cooperated as I opened for him. I was ready to receive him. After a couple of skillful maneuvers, the head of his dick found its own way to my wet opening. Careful not to move to fast he began working his way inside without once having to let go of my hands. I squeezed his hands when I felt him breaking through my tightness.

"Relax baby," he told me. "Breathe. I won't hurt you; I promise."

I didn't believe he was going to hurt me. So I did as he instructed. The more he worked inside me, the more it began to feel so damn good. It felt good to him too because I could hear it in his breathing. His words quivered as he whispered to me, "You feel so good."

He squeezed my hands as he managed to enter deeper into me. I began to moan with each stroke. This wasn't at all like I expected. This was so much more meaningful than most girls made it out to be. This would be a moment I would always remember. He made me feel so wanted, desired, comfortable and so good. It wasn't about him dogging me out and being rough. Hell, I was reliant to say that we were making love. The intensity of it definitely felt like it. The way he held onto my hands, the reassuring kisses, the deep gaze into my eyes, the gentle but long deep strokes. My God! I didn't want it to stop.

"Fuck Neph," Marcos groaned. He kissed me wildly as he picked up the speed and depth.

I wanted more. I began thrusting my hips forward against his. We were in sync creating a rhythm that was unique to what was developing between us.

After a while of deep moaning, grunts, and groans I felt his rhythm stagnate and he buckled. I knew he was cumming especially when he groaned loudly and push deep into me. I didn't want it to end.

Soon he laid still on top of me. His breathing was labored as well as mine. We both tried to regain control of our breathing. Both our hearts pounded wildly. He had a light glisten of sweat on top of his skin.

He didn't say anything as he slowly removed himself from me. He rolled to his back crossing an arm over his forehead. I didn't know if I needed to say anything. He seemed to be in deep thought. Maybe it just sunk in that he just fucked a fourteen-year-old.

———

The following morning, he had me on all fours and fucked me doggy style. This time it was a little more aggressive than the night before. But I took it like a good girl.

Oddly he still hadn't said much to me about what took place between us. We took a shower together and played around a little. He made sure Ada and his other servants provided me with a nice brunch before I left. He did a lot of talking on the phone while I ate. I stayed out of his way. I think one of his calls was to his mother.

Instead of waiting on one of the boys to show up in the white SUV, he drove me home himself in his white Mercedes.

Regardless if this were a one-time thing, I would always remember that weekend as one of the best weekends I've ever had in my life.

Instead of taking me home, he dropped me off at Nikki's as planned.

Before I got out of the car, he reached over and took my hand in his. He studied our hands interlocked for a minute before he spoke. "When can I see you again?"

"Whenever you have the time for me," I said.

"I'll make the time. I just wanna know if you're prepared for what's about to come."

"What does that mean?" I asked.

"It means you can't back out of this now. At this point, it's too late. You're mine, and you betta let every mothafucka that get in your face know that you belong to me."

I didn't need to look at his face to know he was serious about every word he just spoke.

I nodded. "I'm yours, Marcos."

"That's what I wanted to hear. Give me a kiss," he said softly.

We met in the middle and shared affectionate pecks on the lips.

"Call me later," he told me.

"I don't know if you're the busy type," I said.

"It don't matter. Page me. I'll call you back," he told me.

"Okay," I said. I got out of the car and went to Nikki's door. He didn't pull off until he saw me go inside. I didn't know it at the time but what we shared the night before was the beginning of his ownership of me. It was a done deal. I was his property.

Chapter 6

I was young and fresh, and it seemed as if Marcos couldn't get enough of me. I was his every weekend. He never pressured me to be with him any time other than that. He respected the fact that I was still in school and as long as it was still in service, I had to go. I didn't know who he was with during those times. Other girls in school tried to drop slick little shit once they realized I was his new girl. They would try to say how he messed around with this girl and that girl from the neighborhood. I didn't care.

One thing I admired about him was his insistence that I always go to school. He would always say he didn't want a dumb bitch on his side. School was a must; that I really appreciated about him.

I was overly excited when he showed up with his crew to my school's end of year rally where Corvell, Nikki and I danced. Marcos being there to support me put a little extra confidence in my step. And I delighted over the fact that every girl in school was drooling over him and he was mine!

How weird was that? Just weeks before I wasn't thinking of having a boyfriend and here I was with this grown ass man.

Once school was over, I was with him constantly. He respected my closeness with Jovelyn, Corvell, and Nikki; therefore he allowed them to come along most of the time. He even allowed them to sleep over with me at his house. Sometimes Marcos wouldn't be there, but he made sure Ada and the rest of the servants took care of us. He would show up in the middle of the night whisking me off to his bedroom to do what he loved doing best.

Now what was funny was because Marcos was accepting of Corvell, Cory began to bow down to his brother. I asked Marcos why he was comfortable with Corvell when most guys weren't. He told me that Corvell's sexual preference didn't have shit to do with him. But he warned me that Corvell was the only man he would allow around me like that.

But there was still Kenny. For some reason, Jovelyn wouldn't let me sleep alone whenever we were at home. We always slept in the same bed. However, that didn't prevent Kenny from trying to hem me up in the hallway or in the kitchen when no one was around. He would grab me inappropriately, and it was really frustrating.

"Marcos," I said to him one lazy June evening.

"What baby," he said to me.

"There's something I wanna tell you," I said carefully.

He looked back at me. "What is it?"

"It's my stepdaddy," I sighed.

"What about that nigga?"

"He won't leave me alone."

A scowl covered Marcos's face. He sat up fully and asked, "What do you mean?"

"I mean, he's been bothering me inappropriately," I couldn't bring myself to even look him in the face.

"How long has this been going on?"

"Since I was little. He went to prison for a little while, but he came back a few months ago. He still be trying to bother me. He tells me if I say anything that he'll kill me, Jovi, and my mama."

"Why are you just now saying something to me?" Marcos was livid. He jumped up from the sofa in the hearth room.

"Where are you going?" I asked.

"What did you tell me that shit for Neph?" he asked me with fire in his eyes.

"I don't know."

"You told me for a mothafuckin reason," he said angrily. "I'll be back."

"Marcos!" I called out to him. "What are you about to do?"

He didn't respond to me. He disappeared down the hallway. I looked over at Ada in the kitchen. She just shook her head and continued to move about.

When I heard the sound of his truck peeling out, I grew a little nervous. What had I done?

Ada looked over at me and motioned for me to come in the kitchen. I sat at the breakfast bar while I watched her and two others prepare for dinner later.

"How old are you chile?" she asked.

"Fourteen," I answered.

"Do you know Marcos that well?" she asked.

"I know what he wants me to know," I answered honestly.

"Figures. You know that boy ain't wrapped too tight. I love him to death, but he got a few screws loose. You should know that just by the fact he got your little ass up in here screwing you to death every chance he can get. Now I will say this. Not many people get to see the inside of this place. He got other apartments more in the city area, but this place was built by his daddy. His daddy left it for him. Hell, it's bigger than what

Marcos's mama and sister live in. But him and Andrés are just alike. They some mean bastards. I know. I worked for Andrés while he was living over here in the states."

"So where is Marcos's daddy now?" I asked.

"He's in Colombia. That's his home country. He fled from the states years ago. He placed his wife and two kids here 'cause he didn't want nobody to link them together for their safety. His brother was already living here, so Andrés thought this was the perfect place to hide his family out of harm's way. Well, he didn't think his son would get that same itch he got and want to run shit. But Andrés refuse to let Marcos get his hands dirty like his. Marcos do a little dirt but not enough to get him hemmed up by the feds. I think he just like the thrill of it all cause the man got enough 'clean' money to not worry about a thing for the rest of his grandchildren's lives. Cause Andrés done revitalized a whole village down there in Colombia with all the legit business, he done set up there. The only thing is he uses his legit businesses to launder all his dirty money."

"Wow!" was all I could say.

"Now don't say nothing 'less he tell you all this hisself. I just thought you should know. You're such a pretty smart little girl, and I hate to see you get caught up in his mess."

I nodded. She definitely gave me something to think about. But at this point, I wasn't sure I could just walk away from Marcos. The feelings I had for him had grown strong.

When Marcos returned, it was the middle of the night, and the house was quiet. He woke me up by gently rocking me.

"Baby?" he whispered.

"Hmm?"

"I need you."

I smiled and opened my eyes. I knew what that meant. He must have had a stressful night.

Marcos snatched the covers off of me and grabbed me by my ankles. He forced my legs apart and tugged at my panties until they ripped in his hands. Like a drug to soothe his nerves, he needed to eat me. I never turned him down. I let him take care of his addiction until I came in his mouth. It was what he needed most nights. Sometimes penetration wasn't even necessary. But tonight, he needed to relieve some stress, and he tore my ass up.

———————

I soon learned that Kenny had been attacked in a random act of violence and died of multiple stab wounds. I never brought it up, but I speculated that Marcos knew something about Kenny's attack.

Lailani was upset about it the most, but she could see a little peace. Jovelyn wasn't as upset as I thought she would have been. After his burial, she whispered to me, "The boogeyman is gone now."

Was there something she was telling me? All this time her boogeyman was her own father? Had Kenny been touching her too? It made me angry all over again and felt his death was justified.

To help my mama get through this trying time, I opted to stay home with her for a while until she felt better. Marcos didn't like it, but he went on about his business.

So since he thought I was at my mama's, he decided to play around with his other little girlfriends. I know because Nikki called me to inform me that he was messing with some girl in the building over from hers. She was the reason why he had been over there the day I met him. The girl's name was Lisa. With the fat wad of cash Marcos had given me I caught a cab over to Nikki's.

She and I sat on the back of her building breezeway steps and openly spied on the girl's apartment. The white SUV was definitely parked outside of the apartment.

"Who else was with him?" I asked.

"I think only Quan but Ranessa down there with him," Nikki explained.

"And you're sure it's Marcos and not Gogo?"

"Gogo got hair; Marcos don't. I know the difference between the two."

"I should just go down there and knock on the door," I said.

"All he's gonna do is embarrass you," she said. "I mean Marcos cool to an extent. But beyond that, I wouldn't trust his ass. He got too much money to wanna be just tied down with you. Guys like him have plenty of women. You can't even go to a club with him."

She was right.

"Besides, has he said y'all go together?" she asked.

"He's said that I belong to him."

"That's not the same as y'all going together. He can claim you and every other female in this city," she said. "I bet he telling Lisa the same thing."

I wanted to cry. I wanted to believe I was special to him. I shouldn't have given in. My young heart wasn't equipped for it. I was just gonna end it. I got up and took off down the hill to the other apartment building.

"Nephia!" Nikki called out to me. "Don't be stupid!"

"I'm not," I said. "I just want him to know I see him."

"And what's that gonna do?"

Hell, I didn't know. I wanted him to know I was hurt.

I got to 1101K and knocked on the door. I was glad it was pretty early because no one was really out to witness this.

The door opened, and there was the girl. She was a dark-skinned ghetto fabulous girl that I had seen around with Ranessa before. She stood aside with a smirk allowing me a full view of Marcos sitting on her sofa shirtless.

"Marcos, it's your little friend," she taunted.

"Who?" he asked not bothering to even look my way.

Lisa stepped out of the way, so he could see me.

His face frowned up when he saw me standing at the door. His eyes returned back to the television before him. He simply said, "Go back home Nephia."

Really? So this was how he was gonna do me? I wasn't going to argue and make a fool out of myself in front of this girl and Ranessa.

Fuck it! I had to.

"What is this Marcos?" I asked.

"Didn't I tell you to go home?" he snapped.

"I wanna talk to you!"

"I don't. Now get the fuck on," he said angrily.

Lisa snickered finding it all humorous.

Ranessa said, "Damn, why don't her young ass get it? That's why you can't mess with young girls."

Lisa shook her head.

"Marcos?" I queried desperately. I wasn't thinking about Lisa or Ranessa.

I'm not sure what he grabbed from that girl's end table, but I didn't stand there long enough for it to hit me. It shattered once it contacted with the door and the threshold. I could hear Lisa fussing and going off while Ranessa laughed.

Marcos snarled, "Shut the goddamn door on her ass!"

I turned away and walked off like a dog with my tail tucked between my legs. Nikki was right there to console me and let me know it was going to be alright. But it wasn't. Because the day I was telling him about Kenny I should have been telling him I hadn't had a period since we've been having sex. Now I was really messing my life up. All because of his lies.

I didn't even feel like staying and talking to Nikki anymore. I caught a cab back to Cayce. Instead of going straight into the house I walked up to the community center and swung on the swings. I cried for a while and blamed myself for everything. I had to get back focused the way I was before Marcos. But now a baby would be in the picture.

———

After that incident, I didn't hear from Marcos until two weeks later. He showed up at my mama's house early one Sunday morning. He was by himself. He rarely came inside, but he did this time.

"What's your problem?" he asked me. His brow was pinched in a scowl.

"I ain't got one," I said sitting down on my bed placing a pillow over my stomach.

"So why ain't you called me?"

"Why would I call you after you treated me like you did?"

"How did I treat you?"

I cut my eyes at him and sucked my teeth. "Don't be stupid Marcos."

"Neph, I ain't your man, so I don't know why you came to that girl house like that anyway," he explained.

My mouth dropped open in disbelief. "Are you serious?"

"We ain't no fucking couple."

I could feel the burn of tears forming. I pouted hugging my pillow closer. "Okay, we're not a couple. This was why I never wanted to get involved with you or any other boy because all y'all do is break girls' hearts and use them."

"I didn't use you," he said.

"Then what was it, Marcos?"

"Shit, every fuckin thing we did was mutual. You wanted it just as much as I did. Hell, you got compensated for it. So how I use you?" he asked.

I shrugged and lowered my head in sadness. "I guess you're right."

"To be honest, I was never supposed to fuck your little young ass. I fucked up. The shit was wrong, but that young pussy of yours was calling."

I looked at him intently. "So you knew it was wrong to be messing with me?"

"You were too young," he said.

"So what now?" I asked.

"*Usted calcula que mierda fuera niña.* Here, just give me my damn phone and pager back."

My mouth dropped open in disbelief again. Without arguing I retrieved his stuff and threw it at him.

"Hey!" he shouted sternly. "No need for the fuckin attitude. You know I can't keep fucking with you."

"You coulda fooled me!" I cried. "You didn't want another nigga in my face, and I was supposed to be all yours, but you had the freedom to be with whoever you wanted to be with."

"Shut up Nephia," he said annoyed. "Another reason I came by here was to let you know I'm about to go to Colombia for a little while. I don't know when I'll be back."

"Bye," I said with an attitude.

"Fuck you too Nephia," he said nonchalantly. He got up to leave. Before he walked out of my room, he stopped at my chest of drawers. He was messing with something, but I refused to watch him as he walked out of my life. I waited until I knew he had left before I had a fit and broke down crying.

Lailani came into my room. "What's the matter, baby?"

I looked at her and screamed into my pillow.

"You broke up?"

"I don't wanna talk about it Mama," I cried. I got up to look on top my chest of drawers. He left a big knot of money and his chain with the cross that I loved. I didn't know what him leaving it behind meant. Was it some type of peace offering and asking for his forgiveness? I looked at the money. I was sure I had enough money to get twenty abortions. Now the problem was telling my mama so that she could help me get one.

Chapter 7

Another year of school had started and was almost over. I was back focused on my work. I managed to find the joy and laughter in everything as I once had before. Corvell and Nikki were my biggest support. And since drastic changes were happening in our lives, my mama had started doing better. It actually showed in our home life. Jovelyn was a lot happier and healthier. Hell, Lailani had even picked up some weight. We even managed to get a home phone and basic cable.

As time went on, I couldn't deny that I missed Marcos like hell. He was my first love. I don't think I wanted to give myself to another guy as I did with Marcos. But it was sad because he had been gone since the end of June. It was almost time for my Freshman year to come to an end, and I had not heard from him at all. In a couple of months, it would be a year since he left. I saw Quan a few times, but he didn't really speak to me like that.

I wanted to know how he was doing. I wanted to know if he was okay. I wanted to know if he had found him somebody new.

"Hey, Nephia!"

It was the last day of school, and I was saying my goodbyes to some of my classmates. Since arriving at Stratford High School, I had gotten a lot of attention from so many different new boys. Most of them were upper-classmen. I turned down a lot of offers to go to senior and junior prom.

I looked up and saw Kendall approaching me. He was really crushing on me. And if I were still stuck on stupid, I would probably give Kendall a chance. He was cute and athletically built. He was really sweet and was gonna be the star quarterback for next football season.

"You catching a ride with me?" he asked.

"I gotta see what Corvell and Nikki doing," I said.

Kendall smiled showing off his deep dimples. "Boy, I swear. Y'all don't do nothing without the other."

I smiled back, "You know it."

"So what are you gonna get into this weekend?" he asked.

I shrugged. "I'm not sure. I know we were probably gonna go to the skating rink tomorrow for Tamara King's birthday party. It's her sweet sixteen."

"Oh yeah. Me and some of my friends were gonna go check that out too. I heard it's supposed to be off the chain."

"Yeah I heard the same thing," I smiled up at him. "Well, maybe we could see each other there."

He smiled back. "Yeah, that'll be good."

I could hear Corvell's loud mouth before I saw him. "C'mon Nephia!"

"I'm coming!" I yelled. I shrugged at Kendall. "I'll guess I see you tomorrow."

"Yeah," he said.

I could feel him staring at me as I hurried off. Kendall was ideal for me, but I just didn't want to get caught up again.

Corvell looked past me at Kendall. He grinned at me. "Girl, that boy want yo little Asian ass."

"Oh shut up!" I playfully punched him. "Where Nikki at?"

"She waiting on us out on the side," he said. "I hope you got your money cause we 'bout to go shopping bitch."

Corvell was a trip. I could do nothing but shake my head at him most of the time.

And remember the knot of money Marcos had left behind for me? Well, it turned out to be ten thousand dollars. I've been pinching off of it for this whole year now. I paid Mama's bills with it, and we brought extra food when needed. But before Marcos left the ten thousand, I already had a good twenty-five hundred from where he had previously given me a wad of money. So if I ever have the chance to run back into him, I would like to personally thank him for that. And I still had the necklace that wasn't white gold after all. It was platinum and diamonds!

———————

I was actually excited about going to this party. I would have been a while since I really allowed myself to enjoy the social scene. I had been keeping myself busy with school, extracurricular activities, track and field, and home life. My only social interaction was in between bells at school and talking to Corvell and Nikki on the phone.

I decided on a Chicago Bulls Jordan 23 jersey dress. It was cute. I wore my hair down which was rare, so it fell down my back and over my shoulders in its natural wispy fine state. I placed a matching Chicago Bull's snapback cap on my head backward. I placed the diamond necklace around my neck. I put on some cute gold hoop earrings. I slipped on my white footies with red pompoms and slid them into some red Nike Cortez sneakers.

Nikki and Corvell came right on time to get me Saturday. I

said goodbye to my mama and Jovelyn. I told Lailani not to worry or wait up. I gave them all kisses before I left.

This party was already live when we arrived. Everybody was at the Brentwood skating center. It was packed!

Kendall spotted me right away. He complimented me on my look. He said I was cute.

"I ain't never really seen you in a dress though," he said with a laugh.

"I know," I said.

"But you somehow managed to dress that down too," he added.

"It's not too boyish is it?"

"I don't think a boy could come close to looking like you do," he said.

I blushed. This boy was really sweet. Everyone said I should give him a chance. They said we would make a cute couple. I don't know. It depended on how persistent he was.

He and I talked a while before we decided to head out to the rink to get our skate on. I wasn't the best skater, but I enjoyed trying to keep up with Corvell and Kendall. Those boys were so cold on the wheels!

I busted my ass a few times. Kendall was right there to help me to my feet every time. I was having a good time until I saw a figure in all white talking to the birthday girl and her mother. When I saw Gogo and Boogie, I knew the all white was Marcos. Why was he here? When did he get back to the US?

"Nephia?" Kendall was saying to me. He waved his hand in front of my face.

Corvell and Nikki came rushing over to me. Corvell said in a panic, "Bitch, guess who just showed up here?"

Nikki said, "From the looks of it, she just noticed."

I broke out of my trance. "I gotta go. I can't be here if he's here."

"Fuck that," Corvell said. "He don't run nothing. That nigga been gone for almost a damn year. Knowing his retarded ass, he probably been here stalking yo ass from a distance."

"He don't care about me like that," I said.

"Don't go," Nikki said. "Stay here and have fun with us. Ignore his ass. Hell, you here with Kendall anyway."

"Is that dude?" Kendall asked. He seemed a little bothered by the competition.

"Yeah, but he was last year. It's over," I assured him.

"But isn't he the one..." he let his voice trail for me to fill in the blank.

I nodded my answer.

"Don't let him showing up ruin your night," Corvell was saying. He blew an exasperated breath of air. "Aw shit girl, he done spotted yo' ass."

I looked at where he was, and sure enough, he was looking in our direction. Shit! "I gotta go." I hurried off the rink and rushed to the shoe rental to get my shoes back. The boy behind the counter wasn't going fast enough. I could see the mass of white moving closer to me in my peripherals. I grabbed my shoes as soon as the boy placed them on the counter and I ducked around a partition and shot across to the ladies room.

Putting on my shoes in one of the bathroom stalls I

thought I was safe in there. That was short lived when I came out there he was in the ladies room waiting for me. His arms were folded across his chest that looked like it was more swollen than I remembered. His pretty boyish looks were still intact. His hair was a little curlier because it had grown out. But damn! He still looked good in his all white.

I looked at him unsure of what he was thinking. He was showing little emotion. He was just staring at me.

I decided to break the awkward silence. "Hey. I didn't know you were back."

"That's all the fuck you got to say to me?" he asked angrily.

Here it comes, I thought. He done heard some shit! But it wasn't bad; I just knew the type of person Marcos was, and he wasn't going to like what he heard.

"What am I supposed to be saying?" I asked.

"You know what the fuck I'm talking about," he said. He unfolded his arms and walked upon me as if he was about to strike me. "C'mon man. We about to take a ride."

Grabbing me up by my arm he practically dragged me out of the restroom. I tried to pull away, but he wouldn't let me go. He was embarrassing me, and I didn't appreciate it one bit.

Corvell, Kendall, and Nikki rushed over to see what the matter was.

"What are you doing Marcos?" Nikki asked.

"Mind your fucking business!" he snapped.

"Why you handling her like that?" Kendall asked trying to stand up for me.

Marcos didn't even have any words for him. Instead, he

shook me in his grasp and pointed to Kendall. "Is this the nigga you been fucking?"

"No!" I said trying not to cry in front of all of these people.

"And if she was why would you care?" Nikki challenged. "You left buddy!"

"Nikki don't," I pleaded with her.

"Didn't I tell you to stay the fuck out our business!" Marcos spat.

"Okay Marcos," I pleaded with him. "Let's just leave."

"Don't go with him!" Nikki yelled.

I didn't want to cause a bigger scene than it already was becoming. I willingly went with Marcos although he refused to let my arm go.

Surprisingly, Boogie and Gogo didn't accompany him. He was driving a white Lexus SUV now. He literally threw me in the passenger side. I gathered myself as he walked around to the driver side and got in.

"Talk Nephia!" he demanded as he started the car.

"About what?" I asked calmly.

"Don't play mothafuckin stupid with me! You didn't think I would hear about the shit you done while I was gone?"

"First of all Marcos, what I've done while you were away is not your business. You left without so much as caring about me," I said.

He peeled out of the skating center's parking lot missing parked cars by mere inches.

"Can you slow down and where are you taking me?" I

asked.

"I'm taking you home. What the fuck you got on any goddamn way? Don't you think that dress a little too short?"

"My dress is fine."

He scoffed. "What the fuck you wearing my necklace for and you fucking other niggas?"

"I haven't been fucking other—"

And just like that, he smacked me. It really took me by surprise.

"Lie again!" he spat. He went to hit me again, but I cowered covering my face. He balled his fist and punched me in my shoulder instead.

"Marcos!" I cried out. "Please!"

"Whatchu calling my name out for now? Were you calling on me when you was fucking the other nigga?"

"I wasn't fucking no other niggas!" I tried to tell him. He smacked me again. I started crying. "Please stop! I promise I hadn't fucked anybody else."

"I oughta throw your ass out this mothafuckin car while it's moving," he threatened.

"Please don't," I whispered. I wanted to know what he had heard, but I dared not open my mouth to ask.

"You bitches are something else. Can't trust none of y'all asses. That's why I do y'all like I do. None of you bitches know shit about loyalty," he ranted.

"But I do," I said. "That's why I wear this necklace every day."

"Did I ask you to talk?" he shouted.

Why was he flipping out on me? I had never seen this side of him before. I never thought I would. I thought it was best that I stay quiet the remainder of the ride. When he pulled up along my mama's building, I didn't know what he wanted me to do.

"Why you sittin there looking stupid?" he asked me.

"What are you gonna do, Marcos?" I asked.

"We about to see. Get the fuck out the car!"

I couldn't. I didn't know what he was gonna do. "Before we go in here I just—"

He reached over and grabbed me by my neck and pushed my head into the window. "Why the fuck you stalling? The shit is true ain't it Nephia? I oughta fuck yo ass up right here right now!"

I tried to peel his fingers from my neck because I couldn't breathe.

"Get out the goddamn car and take your ass in the house!" he ordered as he released me.

This time I didn't hesitate. I quickly got out of the car and hurried ahead of him to my mama's front door. I let myself in with my key, but he was right behind me.

I think I surprised my Mama because she wasn't expecting me so early. When she saw my face, she became worried. "What's wrong—"

I interrupted her and asked, "Where is she?"

Lailani pointed upstairs. She looked at Marcos behind me with confusion. Seeing the scowl on his face, she didn't say anything.

I rushed upstairs to my room. Again he was right behind me. I went straight to her crib and picked her up in my arms. I turned to him and pleaded, "Please don't be mad Marcos. Please!"

He looked at the baby I was holding. "So you did have a baby while I was gone?"

I started crying. "I didn't just have a baby; I had *our* baby. She's yours."

I backed away from him because I didn't want him hurting the baby.

His face contorted into a confused one. With his head cocked to the side and wearing a frown, he asked, "My baby?"

"She's three months old. Do the math. I was pregnant when you left," I told him. "I promise I hadn't been with anybody else. I promise."

He sat down on my bed, and I could see him doing the math in his head. He looked at his daughter and sighed heavily. He held his head down and rubbed his hand through his hair in frustration. When he looked back up at me, I could see tears welling in his eyes. He asked me again, "My baby?"

I nodded.

"Can I see her?" he asked.

Cautiously I handed her over. She was still sleeping through all of this. He held her out in front of him so that he could get a good look at her. Between the both of us, she was going to be fair skinned. She would have fine hair. When her eyes were opened, they were his exact eye shape. She had my nose, and her lips fell somewhere in between mine and his. She was fifty percent Black, twenty-five percent Asian and twenty-five percent South American. And like everyone predicted, if Marcos and I ever had kids, they would be beautiful. Marcena had proven that.

The look on his face was a mix of awe, sorrow, shock, and joy. He looked at me with tears streaming down his cheeks. He reached out to me, "I'm sorry Nephia. C'mere baby."

I believed he was sorry. He was acting on misinformation that I believed someone told him on purpose. I was just totally shocked that he would treat me that way, but I forgave him instantly.

I went to him and let him pull me into his hold. He told me over and over how sorry he was. I kissed his tears away, and I said, "I know, and I forgive you. And I've never stopped loving you."

He asked, "You love me?"

I nodded. "I've loved you since I gave myself to you."

"You never told me."

"I know. But know that I do now."

"I love you too Nephia. Baby, I promise I do. And I go crazy just thinking of someone else being with you. I'll never do that again. Do you forgive me?"

"I told you I did," I offered him a smile for reassurance.

He looked back down at our daughter. "What did you name her?"

"Marcena," I told him with a smile. "I tried to name her after you, but I couldn't come up with anything that sounded cute."

He smiled. He looked around my room. "It seem like

you've been doing pretty good by yourself."

"I've been using the money you left me," I told him.

"Y'all coming to live with me," he told me with finality.

I wasn't sure if he was serious, so I kept quiet on that. I was just glad to have this misunderstanding cleared up.

————————

So this nigga was serious. The following week, he had a crew moving us out of the projects. Lailani didn't have the opportunity to object. Jovelyn was a little upset because she would be moving away from her friends. And where his house was located, I wasn't zoned for Stratford. But I had my mama get a special transfer so that I could continue to go there.

Lailani fell in love with Marcos's house. She had a room the size of our whole project to herself. And Jovelyn got over missing her friends real quick.

Now mind you I was fifteen now. Since I had his baby, things between me and Marcos had shifted. He convinced Lailani to fill out the paperwork and sign for me to consent to marry him at the age of fifteen. This was a very drastic life-changing event. I wasn't sure if it's what I wanted. He waved a four-carat diamond ring in my face and it kind of changed my mind. He also felt a need to tell me a prenuptial agreement wasn't necessary because I wasn't ever divorcing him. Ever.

After going to court to get consent to apply for the marriage license and waiting the three day waiting period, in the state of Tennessee, I became Mrs. Marcos Delgado Beauchamp on June 20th, 1997.

I didn't know it at the time, but there was a method to Marcos's madness. Ada knew it, but she appeared to be happy for us nonetheless. She was overjoyed that there were more people in the house to look after.

"Baby," Marcos was saying as he was getting dressed.

"Yeah," I said absently as I tended to my own attire.

"Are you nervous?"

"About meeting your mama?" I asked.

"Yeah," he said.

"Well I wouldn't be as nervous about it if you had told her the truth about everything first," I said.

"I know, but I didn't think things were going to work out like this," he said. He looked at the time on his watch. He leaned over to give me a peck on my cheek. "I gotta go, or I'll be late."

"Wait, where are you going?" I asked.

He spoke over his shoulder as he rushed out of our bedroom. "I gotta go pick Andrés up from the airport."

"Andrés?" I repeated to myself. Then it dawned on me. "Marcos! Your father is coming too?"

Marcos was already gone. Oh hell naw! Both parents at the same time! This was going to be one epic family reunion!

After I got myself dressed, I went to see how everyone else was coming along. Jovelyn and Lailani were all dressed and ready. Marcena was cute as always. Ada and the crew had the house smelling delicious.

The security system alerted that there were visitors at the gate. Looking on the monitors, I saw that it was two of my favorite people: Corvell and Nikki. They were actually accompanied by their mothers, Nancy and Tina. I granted them access.

Nikki's little sister, Secret tagged along for Jovelyn. The two girls were thrilled to see one another.

"Ooh, it sho do smell good up in here!" Corvell exclaimed. He went into the kitchen only for Ada to shoo him out.

"Where's Marcena?" Nikki asked.

"Yeah, I wanna see the baby," Nancy said excitedly.

"She's in the cut over there," I said pointing across the hearth room where Marcena was peacefully sleeping in her customized white whickered bassinet.

Corvell pulled me aside and whispered, "Where crazy ass at?"

"He went to pick up his daddy from the airport," I told him.

Corvell gasped. "From Columbia?"

I nodded.

"The drug lord dude?"

I shrugged. "I don't know what he does."

"Oh my God. We finna be in the company of a real crime boss!" Corvell started hyperventilating. "Ooh, chile! Are these windows bulletproof? Who can get through that gate? We got some guns in here? What if these niggas come in here shooting? They gon rob us! They gon kill us all execution style. I can't be here!"

I started laughing. "Boy, if you don't sitcho ass down somewhere!"

Ada shook her head laughing at Corvell. "That boy is a mess!"

More guests had arrived. I looked at the monitors and saw that it was Marcos's entourage with their dates. I was excited to see Bridgette accompanying Gogo. She and I greeted with warm sisterly hugs.

"I hadn't seen you in a while," she said. Like I said she was a really cute girl. She seemed in better spirits than when I first met her. She wasn't mixed like most of the girls the guys had to have on their arms. She appeared to be all black with a light cocoa complexion. She had a really pretty smile with deep dimples. She was taller than me but was thinner than me. Yeah, Marcena had given me more hips and made my ass a little rounder. I didn't mind because Lailani had no ass at all. I was thankful for the Blackwell's genetic contributions.

I made sure to go around and do introductions. Corvell still hadn't calmed down, so I advised everyone to ignore him.

The security system sounded off alerting that someone had entered the passcode and was coming through. When I looked at the monitor, it wasn't a car I was familiar with. It was a black Mercedes.

The guests walked in on their own. All I heard was the thump of heels against the hardwood floors leading to the hearth room and open kitchen.

A very regal brown-skinned woman, skin like chocolate walked in. She had a very elegant look. Her hair was in a short Toni Braxton style that framed her oval face. Her makeup was flawless. She had a flesh mole under her left eye. She was slender built but tall. She wore a lavender sleeveless wrap jumpsuit with Lucite mules. She was well groomed and polished; accessorized all the way down to her toes.

She was followed by a younger girl that looked to be about

my age with the same honey complexion as Marcos's. She had eyes like his too. She wore her hair in a wavy natural style off her face held by a headband. She almost looked like Aaliyah, no lie.

Ada greeted the chocolate woman with a big hug. "Well, how are you, Mrs. Beverly!"

Beverly hugged Ada back. She smiled pleasantly, "I'm doing well. And how are you?"

"I'm good! Why hadn't y'all been out here to check on this old woman?" Ada asked in a teasing manner.

"Well you know, just busy with everything," Beverly said. She looked around at everyone. She smiled. "Hello, boys."

"Hey Mrs. B," Quan greeted. He stood to give her a kiss on the cheek. He ruffled the younger girl's hair playfully. "What's up Chrissy?"

She pushed him away. "Stop it big head." She looked over at Bridgette and smile, "Hey Bridgette. I didn't know you would be here."

Bridgette smiled. "Yeah, I'm here."

Chrissy cut her eyes over at Gogo. "I guess he acting like he got some sense."

Beverly cut around the furniture to approach me, Nikki, Lailani, Tina, Nancy, and Corvell. "I don't believe I know any of you. I'm Beverly, Marcos's mother. You all are?"

Everyone named themselves off one by one. I was last. I looked at her and said, "And I'm Nephia."

It was odd because the mentioning of my name did little for her. There was no sudden realization that she was standing before the young girl that married her son and bore her first grandchild. Even Ada was a little thrown off by that.

I let that pass, and hopefully, when Marcos showed up, he could clear it all. However fifteen minutes passed, and another guest arrived that I wasn't familiar with, but Beverly was. She even went to the door to greet this person. I could hear them gushing over each other. I looked around, and I saw the looks Chrissy exchanged with Bridgette. Bridgette didn't even want to look at me.

Beverly walked in with this gorgeous super sexy vixen with all this long flowing hair down her back. She had booty for days and breast spillage for miles. She had a toasty complexion and a Colgate smile. Like Beverly, her makeup was flawless.

Beverly said with a bright smile, "Everyone, meet my future daughter-in-law, Draya."

Even Gogo, Quan, and Boogie fell awkwardly silent.

I was missing something here. Why hadn't Marcos filled me in on this? I didn't know what to do? As usual, I wanted to cry and deem the evening a disaster. But before I could do that Marcos showed up with two older Latino men and an even older Latina woman.

Before Marcos could show his excitement, I watched his face turn into a frown. He looked at his grinning mother with the Draya chick.

Draya stepped up to Marcos and greeted him with a big hug. "Hey, baby! I've missed you so much!"

What was really going on?

"Why are you here?" Marcos asked without returning the hug.

"What's the problem?" one of the older men asked.

103

Beverly looked at him and smiled, "Hi my darling husband. It would be nice to get an appropriate greeting from you."

"Oh forgive me," Andrés said. He leaned in to peck Beverly on each cheek. The other man followed suit.

"It's so nice to see you, Juan," Beverly said.

Ada walked over and hugged both men and the woman. "It's so nice to see all of you!"

"*Usted todavía alrededor, vieja*?" the old woman said to Ada.

Ada looked at Andrés, "What she say?"

Andrés laughed a hearty laugh. "She called you an old woman Ada."

"Mrs. Delgado knows better," Ada laughed.

So I assumed the older lady was Marcos's grandmother. But I turned my attention back to Marcos and this Draya chick.

"How did you even know about this?" Marcos asked her.

Draya pointed to Beverly. "Your mother. She assumed I was coming."

"But I didn't invite you out here," Marcos said.

Beverly stepped in. "Well Marcos I know you said it was a surprise that you wanted to announce about, you know...marrying Draya. I sort of mentioned it to her when I talked to her the other day."

Marcos closed his eyes as if he was counting to ten. He let out a frustrated breath then opened his eyes and looked at his mother with aggravation all over his face. "I didn't say Draya

Mama! I said Nephia!"

"That's what I thought," Andrés said. He turned to me and said, "Oh forgive me, please. We have not made proper introductions. I am your father-in-law, but you can call me Papa."

I finally was able to smile. "Hi, Papa. I am Nephia, and this is my mother Lailani, and my sister is somewhere upstairs. But these are my friends, Corvell, Nikki, Nancy, and Tina. The baby is over there."

Sofia, the grandmother, bypassed everyone just to get to Marcena. She started speaking in Spanish really fast.

Even Lailani giggled. "What is she saying?"

Beverly wore an expression mixed with shock, embarrassment, and disgust. "Marcos! Are you serious right now?"

"Mama, you don't listen," Marcos said angrily.

"Well, I tried," Beverly said in her defense. "But hell Marcos, you didn't mention anything about a baby!"

"I know I didn't!" he yelled. He looked at Draya, "I'm sorry my mama invited you here like this. But can you leave? I'm sure it would be awkward with you being here."

"Now wait, Marcos," Beverly interjected. "She's here now. She might as well stay."

"But Mama—you know what—Fuck it!" Marcos threw his hands in the air. "This was why I wanted everyone over here today. Nephia is my wife, and we have a baby together. And before you ask, yes she is only fifteen. Ask me if I give a fuck. No, I don't because the state of mothafuckin Tennessee don't give a fuck and allowed me to marry her. Now do what the fuck you wanna do with that. Draya, you still wanna stay?"

Everybody kind of fell into another awkward silence and glanced around with questioning eyes. No one knew about our marriage except me, him, and Lailani. I hadn't even told Corvell and Nikki.

Marcos looked over at Ada and asked, "Is it time to eat?"

Chapter 8

I wanted to know who Draya was, but I didn't bother asking. After Marcos laid everything out for everyone to know, Draya left on her own. She seemed to be hurt and disappointed by the news of Marcos being married to me and having a baby with me as well. I almost felt bad for her because Marcos had no regards for her feelings.

Beverly did not like the idea of what Marcos had done. Not the Draya situation but marrying me and getting me pregnant at the age I was. Andrés shut her up when he reminded her that she was only fifteen when she became pregnant with Marcos. And that was kind of weird to me too. Beverly was Andrés' lawful wife; however, they hadn't lived together as man and wife for several years. Beverly had a beau here in the states, and Andrés had several women he dealt with. I hope that wasn't how Marcos expected us to be.

Other than the awkward introductions, the rest of that evening went about as good as expected. Marcos was in a shitty mood though and snapped at just about everybody.

I was learning Marcos day by day. Living with him was different from just seeing him on the weekends. He was anal about a lot of things. He liked the house to be a certain way. Everything was white, white, white, and more white!

The first year went well. We fell into a routine. I was comfortable. I was happy that my sister and mama were living well now and wanted for nothing. Lailani had become very healthy and had embraced her role as grandmother wonderfully. While Ada made sure the house was maintained properly, Lailani had become an unofficial nanny so to speak.

She loved caring for Marcena. It left me with plenty of time to dedicate to my studies and maintain my four-point zero grade average. It also allowed me to be just as active in school as I was before.

However, something was still missing.

I didn't question Marcos about his whereabouts as long as he came home. If he was going out of town, he always told me about it ahead of time. He kept me informed of his comings and goings. And even while he was away, he constantly checked on us making sure we were okay. When he was home, he spent a great deal of time spoiling Marcena. I had to give it to him; he was a great father. He took pride in being a father. But there was something different that I couldn't quite put my finger on. It was the way he looked at me sometimes. He had a way of looking at me like I disgusted him. I was beginning to believe he didn't love me anymore. He rarely told me.

I was sixteen now. My birthday had been one of the best. Marcos made sure of it. I even got a brand-new BMW, and of course, it had to be white. I didn't argue with him. I accepted every gift he gave me with no complaints. For the first time, other girls were envious of my life. Marcos kept me nicely dressed, money in my pocket, I had the best of everything, and I blinged from head to toe. People talked about me of course, but I didn't care. My family was happy, and that was all that matter to me.

"But are you happy?" Nikki asked me.

I wasn't, but I couldn't understand why. I had everything a girl could possibly ask for. I shrugged. "I guess it doesn't matter."

"What do you mean?" she asked me. She turned to me

with a look of concern on her face. "You should be happy."

We were at the mall as usual. We had taken a break and was eating at one of the tables in the food court. I halfheartedly gnawed on a French fry, "I should be, but sometimes I don't feel it. I mean, I love that Jovi, Cena, and my mama are happy."

"Why are you not happy though?"

"I think it's Marcos. I think he doesn't wanna be married to me anymore."

"Well, he shouldn't have never married you in the first place ol' pervert!" she huffed. She saw that I was annoyed by her statement, so she softened. "I'm sorry. I still think it was odd that he done that. But if you ask me, I think he only done it as a way to control you."

"How is that?" I wondered.

"A guy like Marcos likes power. He loves the power he has over you."

"But he didn't have to marry me for that."

"No, he didn't. I think he also married you to make it look better on his part. That way he could legally screw an underage girl on a regular basis."

"So you don't think any of his motives are genuine when it comes to me?" I asked.

She shook her head slowly as she considered what she would say next. "I'm not saying that. I mean, it's obvious he has something for you. He takes damn good care of you."

"Yeah, but that's it," I said sadly. I tried to remember the last time he and I actually enjoyed one another. It had been a while. Sex was always there but the small intimate quality time was missing.

"So what do you want from him Nephia?" Nikki asked me.

I shrugged. "I want more attention I guess. He comes and goes all the time. And when he's home, he's more into Cena than he is into me. And he's very distant and preoccupied whenever it's just the two of us in the room."

"Talk to him about it. Maybe he doesn't realize what he's doing."

She had a point. Maybe that was the case. Hell, we were married. It wouldn't hurt to try talking to him.

———————

Later that night, I waited up for him. He came in around eleven. He didn't acknowledge me even though he saw that I was still awake. He had his phone up to his ear and was talking low. Immediately, I knew it wasn't one of his friends he was talking to because of the soft tone of his voice. He even laughed a little. His word usage was that of a teasing flirty nature. Was he talking to a woman in my presence?

Instead of taking a shower like he normally would, he was actually gathering some clothes and placing them in an overnight bag.

I was very confused. I jumped out of bed and approached him in his walk-in closet. I stared at him questioning him with my eyes. He never wavered as he continued to hold his conversation and pack his bag.

"Marcos?" I finally questioned.

He said into the phone, "Hey, let me get off this phone and handle something real quick. But I'll see you in a few."

What? Who was he about to see in a few?

Ending the call, Marcos looked at me as if I had ruined his day. "What?"

"That's what I wanna know," I stated. I looked at his bag. "Where are you going?"

"Don't question me Nephia. How many times I gotta tell you that?"

Ignoring him, I said, "I know you're not leaving."

"And if I am?" he countered.

"But where? It's eleven at night."

"I got some business to take care of," was all he said. He went to grab the bag, but something in me refused to let him leave. I snatched it from him.

"No!" I said firmly. I didn't want to accept what was happening but deep down I knew what it was without him having to say it. I looked up at him desperately and asked, "Is it another woman you're going to?"

Marcos wasn't trying to hear that. He snatched his bag back from me and shoved me out of the way. "Go on Nephia. Take yo ass back to bed."

"But what did I do wrong, Marcos?" I cried.

"What the fuck you mean?"

"Why are you doing this to me?"

"I haven't done anything to you yet," he said. I could hear the threat in his voice.

"But you're leaving home to go be with another woman."

"Where the fuck you think I am all the other times?" he asked me as if I was stupid.

Was he admitting to me that he was seeing other women?

I swallowed the hard lump that had formed in my throat. "Are you cheating on me, Marcos?"

"Yeah," he answered without hesitation. He gave me a daring look. "And tonight, I'm going over there."

I didn't know what else to do but cry. His brutal honesty hit me hard and drained my spirit so fast. I let my body drop to the floor and sobbed my heart out. Marcos simply stepped over me and exited the closet.

———————

Conditioning me to believe I wasn't good enough started early I guess. It was during this time I began to doubt myself. Instead of being angry with him, I blamed myself. I wanted to prove to him that I was just as good, or I was worthy of his love too.

I tried to be obedient. I didn't suffocate him. I let him treat me however he wanted to, to prove to him I was committed to him for the long haul. So I let him come back to me when he was ready. He always came back to me. In my young mind, I thought I was winning when in reality I was losing.

When he left that night, he stayed away for an additional two more nights. On the fourth night, he came home and crawled into bed with me like nothing had ever happened. He still didn't touch me. At that point, it had been about two weeks since he had had sex with me. I desired to be with him, but I would let him make the first move.

Marcos continued to keep me at a distance though. I didn't know what he wanted me to do. Getting frustrated with the situation, I decided to put it all aside and enjoy a weekend out with my friends. That was something I hadn't done in a while.

Marcos had left me in the house again anyway.

I jumped in my car on a Saturday night and scooped my two best friends up. Corvell knew of a party happening that Cory had told him about. That was our destination for that night.

When we arrived at the party, I was glad I had chosen to go. I saw a lot of friends from school and was having a good time.

"Nephia," Kendall greeted me with his cute dimples.

I smiled back and gave him a hug. "What's up?"

"I hadn't been seeing you this summer. Where you been hiding?" he asked.

I could barely make out what he was saying because of the music and all the other noise. I led him to the kitchen where it was a little quieter. "I hadn't been hiding. Aren't you getting ready to go soon?"

"Yeah," he said. "We start practice soon."

"I'm really proud of you," I beamed. Kendall had gotten a full football scholarship to UT Knoxville. He deserved it too. Through it all, Kendall had remained a good-natured guy. I had never seen him any other way.

"How's the baby?" he asked.

"She's getting big," I told him. "She's walking now and everything."

"I would like to see her before I leave," he said. He smiled down at me, and I could see there was something more in his eyes.

"What is it?" I asked.

He shook his head wearing a modest smile. "Nothing. I just wish you, and I could have...well, you know."

I giggled. "Yeah, I know. But we're good friends."

"How's dude been treating you?"

I shrugged. "I'm living good."

Kendall's smile faded into a look of concern. "I wish I could make you happy."

I tried to hold my smile, but I could feel the sadness taking over. "I'm good."

I saw Kendall's eyes focus on someone behind me. Before I could turn around, I heard a whisper in my ear, "Heads up. You've been reported."

As soon as the person walked away from me, I turned to see who had actually said it to me. I giggled when I saw that it was Chrissy, my sister-in-law. I didn't even know she was at the party. Chrissy had ended up being cool although she was a spoiled brat. Beverly got on her nerves just as much as she got on everyone else's. Andrés got Chrissy anything she wanted. Marcos did his share of spoiling her too. Chrissy loved her brother, but she knew he wasn't always right. Often times she sided and sympathized with me.

Now, what did she mean by I've been reported? Was Marcos here at this high school house party? Surely he wasn't. And who was here to report anything on me except Chrissy?

"Is everything okay?" Kendall asked.

"Yeah," I said as I looked around. I didn't see anything unusual, but I was paranoid nonetheless. I suggested he follow me out to my car. We weren't the only people outside as others had found their way outside of the house as well. I spotted

Corvell talking to a group of people in the driveway.

For more privacy, we ended up walking down to where I had parked my car along the front yard of one of the neighbor's houses. We talked about some of everything. It was a joy talking to Kendall. Something told me that he was the one I probably should have ended up with. And I knew we would probably cross paths again.

I should have taken heed of what Chrissy said. But she said it so fast and kept going I didn't know if she was really serious. My heart dropped when I saw Marcos's truck pull up to my car. It literally was parked in the middle of the street as an angry Marcos jumped out of the passenger side.

Fearful for Kendall, I nudged him, "Go on."

Kendall wasn't budging. I know he thought we were innocent and we weren't doing anything wrong. We were just two friends talking outside leaning on my car. But not to Marcos.

"Who the fuck told you, you could go anywhere?" Marcos asked me as he walked up into my space.

I backed into my car as far as I could go. "I thought it would be okay."

"With who?" Marcos asked.

I was growing nervous. He was already drawing attention to us just from his presence alone.

"You weren't home, and I didn't want to bother you," I said in a small voice.

Marcos glared in Kendall's attention. "Why every time I catch your ass doing shit you ain't supposed to, this nigga be in your face?"

"He's just a friend," I told him.

"Yeah, we're just friends—" Kendall was saying.

Marcos snapped on him. "I didn't ask you to talk nigga! As a matter of fact, take your punk ass on away from what's mine! Get the fuck away from her and don't let me catch you in her goddamn face again!"

As he was talking, he was inching closer to Kendall. The last thing I wanted was for Marcos to assault Kendall. So I grabbed Marcos's hands and tried to soothe him. "Baby, he's leaving. And I won't talk to him ever again. Can we just go home?"

"I'm so sick of you," Marcos growled through gritted teeth as he jabbed his finger in my forehead.

"But I didn't do anything!" I yelled as I smacked his hand away from me. Oh, why did I do that? I saw how thrown he was in his eyes. Before he could react, I hurried to put about a yard between us. It didn't stop him from coming after me though. I wanted to run because I knew once he got his hands on me, I was going to feel his wrath.

"Don't hurt me, Marcos," I begged. We were about three houses down the street now.

"I'm not gonna hurt you," he told me. His eyes said differently. "But I need you to get in your car and go the fuck home."

"Okay, I will," I said. I kept my distance. I didn't need him embarrassing me more. People were waiting for more drama. At this point, it just looked like we were quarreling and he was trying to get me to talk to him.

"Now Nephia!" he ordered.

"Okay," I said nervously.

"If you don't stop walking you're gonna regret it," he threatened.

"What are you gonna do to me?" I was scared.

"Nothing," he said impatiently. "You think you can really outrun me? I could have already done something to you if I wanted to. I just want you to get out of the street, go to your car, and go home to our baby."

"That's all?" I wanted to trust him. He seemed pretty mad at first. Marcos doesn't calm down that quick.

"That's all," he assured me. He held his hand out to me. "C'mon and we'll talk on our way home."

I reached for his hand. His hand closed around mine a little too tight. He pulled me into him with his left hand at the same time his right hand balled into a fist and socked me right in the nose. It happened so fast I'm sure no one caught what he did.

I could feel blood leaking from my nose, but I was so dazed from the blow I could literally see stars floating around me. Now keep in mind, he punched me at the same time as he was pulling me into him. He was still holding onto me to keep from actually falling to the ground because at this point I was slipping out of consciousness.

Marcos held me close to him as if we had made up and walked me back to my car.

"Where are y'all going?" Nikki asked. She had come outside to see what was going on.

Marcos was placing me inside my car in the passenger seat. "I'm taking her home."

"But we came with her," Nikki stated. She tried to come around to talk to me, but Marcos stopped her.

"Boogie'll take y'all home," he told her.

"I just wanna tell her bye then," Nikki said hatefully.

I could hear this, but that blow still had me out of it. I heard commotion on my side of the car, and I lifted my head to see Nikki trying to get my attention. Her eyes widen when she saw me. I heard her yell at him, "What did you do to her Marcos!"

"Nikki, stay the fuck out of our business," Marcos warned.

"Did you hit her?" Nikki asked. She didn't care who was around listening. She was livid.

I think Marcos decided to ignore her because the next thing I knew, the car was moving. On the drive home, he was yelling at me and cursing me out the whole time. I just wanted him to shut up, so I didn't encourage him to talk by remaining quiet.

I convinced myself that with Marcos bad attention from him was better than no attention. It was a really crazy notion of mine, but this was how I coped with living with him.

Corvell called me the following evening to check on me.

"I didn't know what was going on," he said. "Hell, how that nigga even know where you were?"

"I don't know. All I know is Chrissy, his sister came up to me and told me I had been reported, but then she disappeared."

"Was it her?"

118

"I don't think so."

"You know who probably was running their damn dick suckas? Ladonna an'nem. I saw 'em eyeballing you and Kendall talking," Corvell said. "Let me find out it was they ass. I'ma snatch every single one of 'em bald head."

I giggled. "You can't be doing that Corvell."

"People kill me," he groaned. He said, "Oh, and have you heard about Kendall?"

"No. What about Kendall?" I asked with concern.

"He was in some accident today or something. My brother was telling me about it. Said his football career might be over with already."

I gasped. "Are you serious? Oh my God! What happened?"

Corvell scoffed. "Marcos happened if you ask me."

"Corvell!"

"Don't be stupid Nephia."

"Why would you think Marcos would have anything to do with what happened to Kendall?"

"Cause it's the type of nigga Marcos is. Besides, it was how Cory was telling me. He didn't have to say Marcos's name for me to get it."

"Let me call you back," I said rushing him off the phone. I ended the call with him and quickly called Marcos.

"Hello?"

"Where are you?" I asked.

"Taking care of business. Why?"

"When will you be back home?"

"Why?"

"I'm just gonna ask you straight out. Did you do something to Kendall?"

"You're a dumb ass hoe," was all Marcos said before he hung up in my face.

Needless to say, that dumb ass question I asked warranted me an ass whooping when he got home that night. It also confirmed that Marcos was the one that ended Kendall's football career.

Chapter 9

Marcena was turning two, and I wanted her to have an amazing party. The only thing was her birthday was in February. Not only was it cold outside, but it was the day after Valentine's Day. Since her actual birthday fell on that Monday, I decided to throw her a huge birthday party at our house that Saturday before.

I played perfect hostess to the children in attendance. I catered to their every need while Marcos kept the adults entertained. I wish he had been a little more involved with helping me with the kids. I had Jovelyn, Nikki, my mom, Chrissy, and Ada helping me out, but I would have preferred him helping me as a family.

"Are you okay Nephia?" Chrissy asked me.

I continued with prepping the cake. "I'm fine."

"You look a little sick," she said. She stepped in and pushed me aside. "I'll carry the cake out there. Why don't you go have a seat for a minute?"

Lailani came up to me and placed her hand on my forehead. "You sick?"

I shook my head although I felt like I would pass out. "I'm okay."

Nikki came into the kitchen laughing. "Those kids are ready for some cake!"

"Here we come," Chrissy said. "Where's the lighter for the candle?"

I went to follow Chrissy and Nikki out of the kitchen, but Ada grabbed me by my arm. She didn't say anything to me.

121

She just gave me this knowing look as if I knew what she was saying to me. I think I did, but I wasn't in the mood to confirm it.

I walked away to go find Marcos, so he could at least be present to sing Happy Birthday to his daughter. First of all, I didn't understand why he was so far away from the party in a whole different area of the house. Secondly, why were there so many adults present at a two-year-old's birthday party?

I found them in the downstairs game room. A few were actually at our two-lane bowling alley, and the others surrounded the pool table. There were men and women present drinking, smoking, and snorting. I was not happy about it. I was beginning to really dislike the people Marcos kept around him.

I approached Marcos at the bar where I knew he had just done a line of coke. I could see it in his eyes. I had to be careful in how I talked to him when he was on that stuff. This was when he was the most aggressive. Therefore, I had to pretend the big-boned heifer hugged beside him was invisible.

"Hey baby, we're about to sing Happy Birthday to Cena," I said sweetly. "You know she wants Daddy there."

"I'll be up there in a minute," he told me.

I stood there and stared at him for a second. I really wanted him to be present, but I knew he wasn't going to come upstairs. I tried again. I reached out for his hand and smiled, "We're about to do it now. I don't want you to miss it."

He looked as if I had gotten on his last nerve. He jerked his hand away from mine, turned to the girl, and pecked her on the lips. He said, "I'll be right back."

That shit really hurt. It was embarrassing and humiliating.

And I wasn't feeling good, and something in me just snapped. Before I knew it, I had smacked the shit out of him. I yelled, "I hate you!"

Why did I do that? Lord help me!

The way he looked at me was enough for me to piss my pants, but I refused to cower under his glare. Before I could run away, he had me by my throat by both hands, and my feet were off the floor. Gogo and Boogie fought with him to release me. Some of the women that were present were begging him to let me go. That's all I remembered.

I fell in and out of sleep, but I knew I was in bed. A part of me didn't want to wake up. I laid there wishing I could disappear. Whenever someone came into the room to check on me, I pretended to be asleep. I missed the rest of my daughter's birthday party.

This wasn't supposed to be my life. I thought I had won, but I was losing more and more with each day. I hated myself for not having more control. I hated myself for not thinking I was good enough without Marcos now.

I sat up in my bed. It was dark outside. I wasn't sure who was still in my house. I didn't care because I wasn't going to show my face.

I went to my bathroom and stared at my reflection in the mirror. Marcos choked me so hard, it left bruises around my neck. Although I was already blacked out, when he let go of my neck he still punched me for good measure. My eye was throbbing, but it wasn't swollen shut. There was a nice cranberry colored bruise right under it though.

I started crying uncontrollably until I made myself sick. I stood over the toilet retching, but nothing was coming out. I hadn't eaten or drank anything all day.

The house was quiet and still when I finally decided to leave out of the room. Passing through the kitchen, I noted the time. It was almost ten at night. I couldn't believe I had spent all evening in my room.

I made my way to Cena's bedroom to check on her. She was tucked in her bed clutching her newest doll. I kissed her on her forehead before exiting. I passed my mama's room and noticed she was still awake. She rushed to her door and called out to me.

"You okay Nephia?"

I looked back at her and nodded. "I'm fine."

"You didn't eat. Ada got something for you downstairs. You need to eat," she told me.

I simply nodded and kept going.

I was shocked to see Marcos in the media room watching television alone. It was Saturday, and I just knew he would be out. He was comfortable in only a white t-shirt and white gym shorts. He didn't look like he had any intentions of leaving either.

I went further into the room until I was sure he saw me. He didn't acknowledge me, but his eyes shifted towards me the closer I got to him. I didn't say anything. He allowed me to sit next to him. I just wanted him to love me again.

Taking a chance, I wrapped my arms around him and placed my head on his chest. He didn't move away, nor did he push me away. When his arm wrapped around me and pulled me closer, I smiled on the inside.

Marcos kissed the top of my head and whispered, "I'm

sorry."

I raised up to look at him. He gently touched the tender area below my eye.

"Damn, I'm sorry Nephia," he repeated.

I could tell he was messed up by what he did. His apologies were sincere. They always were after he took inventory of the damage he had done.

"It's okay," I said to him.

"No, it isn't. I love you too much to be doing shit to you like this," he said. "I'm fucked up Nephia, but sometimes I can't help it. You make me mad, and I just react."

All I heard was him saying he loved me. "You still love me, Marcos?"

"Of course, I do," he said. He frowned, "Why wouldn't I?"

I shrugged, "Sometimes I don't feel like you do anymore."

"I do love you. I'll always love you. You're my wife. I chose you. So, no matter what you think I'm doing, know that my heart is always here with you. Ain't nothing or nobody coming between that. You understand?"

I nodded. He started kissing me with intense passion. My heart beat wildly and that connection I once felt a long time ago with him filled me and runneth over. Before I knew it, he had me laid back on the sofa naked from the waist down making me squirm as he feasted upon my love juices.

I was always uncomfortable when we had sex in the house other than our bedroom. He loved it. He had taken me in just about every corner of the house. I was always afraid we would get caught which we had a few times.

He bent me over on the sofa and pounded me from behind. It felt so damn good. When it came to sex, he was always loving and gentle. His strokes were driven by passion and not anger or frustration. He always whispered comforting words to me as he drove his dick deeper into me. I felt the love when we were having sex.

After he got his first nut, he backed out of me and slapped my ass. "C'mon. Let's go to the room."

I happily and eagerly obliged. And for the moment it felt like it did when we very first started messing around. I would run from him as if I didn't want to submit to his sexual needs. He would chase after me and carry me to his bedroom. I would laugh the entire time while giving him a hard time. Those were the days.

When we made it to the bedroom, his erection had started to go down. I didn't hesitate to bring him back to life with my newly learned oral skills.

"Baby," he groaned. He grabbed a handful of my hair and pulled me off of him. For a minute I thought I was in trouble. I thought he was about to hit me. Instead, he kissed me aggressively. He pushed me back onto the bed and held my legs apart so that he could find solace there.

I gasped and moaned as he entered me once again. His eyes closed, and he lost himself as he always did whenever he made love to me.

After he came a second time, he just laid there on top of me. I lovingly caressed his back. I thought this was as good as time as ever to say what I said next.

"I'm pregnant."

At seventeen, going into my senior year of high school I gave birth to twin boys. Marcos was ecstatic. Words couldn't describe how happy he was about his boys. I wanted to be happy too. I faked it. During the pregnancy, Marcos had avoided me like the plague. It was a high-risk pregnancy, and I was placed on bed rest early on. I couldn't even have sex after the third month. Instead of being there for me and suffering through it as well, Marcos continued to do him.

Marcos spent more time at the condo close to town than he did at the house. No one had to tell me, but I knew he had plenty of women keeping him company. I was sad and depressed the entire eight months.

"Why you named them that?" Corvell asked. He was snickering.

"Because that's how I feel," I said sadly. I looked over at the two glass bassinets that contained my babies. Corvell had come to visit me at the hospital. We were standing outside the NICU looking at them through the window. I had just left out of there after their feeding. For the most part, they were healthy. They were a little underweight and was having trouble maintaining the proper body temperature.

"Bleu and Azul?" Corvell asked. "Does Marcos know you named them after a crayon color?"

"He doesn't care," I said flatly.

"Where is he?"

I shrugged. I hadn't seen Marcos since I pushed Bleu and Azul out.

"He's pitiful," Corvell said shaking his head. "So when are you gonna be able to return to school?"

"I guess by the end of September," I said. I looked closely at Corvell's neck and noticed a bruise. Any other person would have assumed it was a passion mark, but I was familiar with the way bruises looked.

"What happened to your neck?" I asked.

His hand subconsciously went to his neck and covered the mark. Uneasiness settled over Corvell and tried to dismiss it as if it was nothing by shaking his head.

"Did Cory do that to you?"

"No," Corvell said with a slight laugh.

"That's not a passion mark Corvell," I said. "Who did that to you if Cory didn't?"

"It's nothing," he insisted. He offered me an empty smile. "C'mon, let's get you back to your room."

I was still sore and moving slow, but I was determined to snap back into shape. I didn't have time to be laying up and letting the fat just accumulate.

I waited until my room door was closed before I went in on Corvell again. "What's going on and you better tell me the truth! Who's putting their hands on you?"

"It's no big deal," he said.

It was sad because he sounded like me. I asked, "Was it the guy you were seeing?"

Corvell sat down at the foot of my bed. "He gets a little crazy."

"A little?" I questioned. "That on your neck don't look a little crazy."

"We had a fight the other night," he said.

"And he had to hit you?"

Corvell turned his lips up at me. "You're one to talk."

"Well just because it happens to me doesn't mean I want it to happen to my friends," I stated. I sat down beside him. "What happened?"

"I sort of threatened to tell his girlfriend about us," Corvell said meekly.

I threw my hands in the air. "Now why would you do that?"

Corvell shrugged. "Shit, I don't know Nephia. I really love him, but he don't want nobody knowing about us."

"Why do you mess around with down low dudes anyway?" I asked. "They're dangerous."

"Cause it's what I like," he said.

"Why don't you find someone more like you who's open with his sexuality?"

"Why don't you find someone who's more like you who know how to treat people?" Corvell retorted smartly. I couldn't even be mad at his comeback.

"It seems like we're both in messed up situations," I responded.

"But I hate Marcos," Corvell said. "You're too good for him. He treats you like garbage while he does whatever with whoever. And now you got three kids by this nigga."

"Corvell, you're not making sense right now. Isn't that what dude is doing to you?"

"But at least I ain't got no kids by his ass!"

I laughed because that was hilariously impossible anyway.

About ten minutes later, Nikki and her cousin Penny showed up bearing gifts. Nikki was out of breath. "Girl, I had to go to two different Targets cause I had to make sure they both got the same thing."

"Thank you but you know they got enough already," I told her.

"I know, but I'm their Godmother so I gotta take care of my babies too," Nikki said. She looked around the room. "Where are they?"

"They had to go back to the nursery," I said.

"Where's Marcos's retarded ass?" Nikki asked.

"Your guess is good as mine," I mumbled.

"Well, I can't stay too long," she said. She started grinning. "Tomas and I are going out tonight."

Corvell started teasing her. "You finally gonna give him some girl?"

Nikki shrugged. "Maybe."

Penny shook her head. "She ain't gon' do nothing."

"She still holding onto that virginity," Corvell said.

"Y'all want me to be all loose like y'all," Nikki laughed.

Corvell pointed to me. "She real loose. She done had three babies pass out her vagina!"

"Shut up Corvell," I said rolling my eyes.

Nikki said, "And remember what Nephia used to always say? I ain't losing my virginity until I'm thirty and married."

"Hey, I got half of it right though," I joked.

Nikki stepped up to me and flipped my ponytail. "Who would have thought you'd be a mother and a wife at the age of seventeen?"

Penny said, "But she got it made though."

Corvell, Nikki and I exchanged glances. We shared the same knowing look. I had it made alright. It also came at a cost.

I was shocked when Marcos walked into the room with Boogie, Gogo, and Bridgette. I looked at her stomach and noticed she was way out there. She had to be ready to deliver her and Gogo's baby any time.

"What's up y'all?" Gogo greeted. He came up to me and placed a kiss on my cheek. "You're looking good cuzzo. Don't even look like you just had twins."

"Thanks," I told him.

"Hey Bridgette," Nikki said. "It's your turn next ain't it?"

"Yeah and I can't wait," Bridgette said in her small voice.

Corvell rubbed his stomach and joked, "Then I'm next!"

Marcos turned his nose up in disgust. "Man, go 'head on with that gay shit!"

Corvell giggled. He got a kick out of messing with Marcos and his crew. Surprisingly, Marcos tolerated Corvell for some odd reason.

Boogie shook his head. "That nigga sick."

Corvell cut his eyes at Boogie and made a face.

"Where're my sons?" Marcos asked.

"They came and got them earlier. They in the NICU," I told

him.

"Why?"

"They were cold," I said. "Do you still have the wristband on? You can go down there to see them."

"Will I be able to hold them?" Marcos asked.

I nodded.

Nikki said, "Well let me go. I'll see you tomorrow Nephia. Bye y'all."

"I'm finna walk with y'all," Corvell said.

Boogie followed behind them. "Let me holla at you Penny."

Marcos gave me a quick peck on the lips. "I'll be back."

I watched him, and Gogo walked out of the room. It was just me and Bridgette.

"So how is it?" Bridgette asked.

"How is what?"

"Being a mother? You've seem to do it so effortlessly."

I half shrugged. "I don't know. It just comes naturally I guess. But I got a lot of help too."

"Yeah, I know. Gogo's mama said she would help me out with the baby so I can keep going to school," she said.

"That's good. Auntie Carolyn is good like that," I told her.

"Isn't this your senior year?"

I nodded.

"Are you going to school afterward?"

"Definitely. I wanted to go to Spelman with Nikki, but I guess I'll be here," I said.

"Of course. Marcos wouldn't have it any other way," Bridgette said.

I fell quiet as I thought about how the plans I had laid out for me years ago had somehow dissipated. My life had been molded into what Marcos wanted for me. I appreciated that he was supportive of me pursuing my education though. He always reminded me that not only did he want me to remain beautiful at his side, but I had to be smart too.

"Do you have any regrets?" Bridgette asked.

My eyes shifted to her. "I try not to think about them."

"I can understand that," she said softly in thought.

I asked her, "Is Gogo as bad as Marcos?"

Bridgette looked at me. Her eyebrows raised as she offered me a dumb smile. "Just about."

My heart went out to her. I felt her pain. The difference between Gogo and Marcos was Gogo beat on Bridgette behind closed doors. He would verbally snap on her in front of people, but that's where it stopped. The very first day I met her, he had physically attacked her just moments before. That's why she had been looking sad that day.

All of the Delgado men were abusive. It was in their blood. They were fine and nice to look at. They had money and came from a well-known family. But they were vicious with their hands.

I told her, "It'll get better."

She said, "I seriously hope so."

Chapter 10

The world didn't come to an end at the turn of the century like everyone was in fear of. I was kind of hoping it would have. Some days I didn't feel like living at all. Other days I barely made it. I was exhausted.

As time went on, I fell into my role of good wife, mother, daughter-in-law, sister and friend. I learned to keep Marcos satisfied enough to minimize the physical abuse. I ended up graduating high school as the class valedictorian despite my home life.

I gave birth to another girl two years after the twins were born. Her name was Yanna. I didn't get to enjoy her as much because I ended up pregnant within weeks of having her. The following year, I gave birth to yet another set of twins. At this point, I didn't know whether I was coming or going. Marcos and I weren't on the best of terms because again he was doing his own thing in the streets.

But here I was the mother of six kids all under the age of six, and I was only twenty. I didn't have time to gain weight. Hell, I think I lost more weight than I gained. I never had time for myself. I was always on the go, and one of my kids were always hanging off of me demanding something. Marcos spoiled the hell out of them, but he hardly stayed around to take some of the load off of me. Yet he expected for me to maintain this perfect image.

Again, Corvell asked me why I named the twin girls what I named them. I pointed outside. Marcos was sloppy drunk when it was time for me to give birth to the girls. He was of no assistance to me. Corvell stepped up and was everything I needed Marcos to be for me while I was in labor. Marcos was passed out on the bench in the delivery room.

I was upset and cried in sync with the awful weather taking place outside. It was storming, and the rain poured down in angered waves. I named the older of the two Stormi and the other one I named Raiyne. And they were feisty too.

I busied myself caring for my six kids, going to school, and helping Beverly out at the fine arts school. I enjoyed the school. It was there that I got to lose myself and block everything else out. Though Nikki went off to Atlanta to go to school, Corvell remained behind with me. He dedicated a lot of time to the school as well.

What bothered me about Corvell though was how he kept his men a secret. He would never tell me their names. He was still seeing the one that got physical with him a few years back, but that wasn't his main boyfriend. He had taken an interest in an openly gay guy that worked at the school as a music instructor named Omar. I thought they were cute together, but Corvell was still drawn to the no good down low men. That one guy really had a hold on him. I wanted to know who it was.

One day when I was on my way home, I decided to swing by Corvell's place unannounced. When I pulled up to his apartment building, I regretted showing up. If what I was seeing was correct, I was immobile with fear of confirming the truth. I looked to the right of me and a few cars down was Marcos's cocaine white Escalade. It was his. Everybody knew it was his. His plates read Marcos 1.

Why was Marcos parked in front of Corvell's apartment? Was Marcos down low and fucking my best friend too? I didn't even want to wait around for the answer. I backed out and left as quickly as I showed up.

I was a mess when I got home. I was pacing back and forward. I had no one I could confide in about this because Corvell was fucking my husband and he was the one that I ran to about everything.

I decided to keep it to myself and would later confront both of them together. Surely Marcos would allow me to go my way after this. He was sick! And Corvell! I didn't know if I could ever consider him a friend again. He knew what I was going through with Marcos. Why? How could he do something like this to me?

Marcos came home and was in a good mood. He was playful with me, but I wasn't feeling it. I could have sworn I smelled dick and ass on him. I was so mad, and I had an attitude.

"What's wrong with you?" Marcos asked.

"Nothing," I mumbled.

"Something's wrong," he said. He grabbed me by my waist and pulled me down with him on the sofa.

"I'm okay," I said.

Marcos reached for my ponytail and started loosening my hair from its holder. "What have I told you about this damn ponytail?"

"I was at the school earlier," I told him.

Azul came running in the hearth room with Marcena chasing him. She was angry and yelling at him. He was laughing.

"Give it back!" she cried. She stopped in front of us and whined, "Daddy, Zuli won't give me my Barbie shoes back!"

Azul stopped on the other side of the sofa in a taunting

stance. He said, "What?"

"It's for girls. You're a boy, and boys can't play with that!" She said.

"Zuli, what have I told you about that gay shit?" Marcos said to him.

Azul held up the plastic pink miniature high heels. "But they isn't shoes Daddy! They guns!"

"Those are shoes boy," I interjected. "Now hand them back to your sister."

Instead of handing them to Marcena he tossed them to her.

"You pick those up, and you place them in your sister's hand," I ordered firmly.

Azul looked to Marcos to see if he cosigned with me. My boys were learning to be bullies early, but I was trying to break them of it before they ended up like their father. Marcos was always okay with them being mean to other kids. But that gay comment he made, made me cringe at how hypocritical he was.

Azul did as I told him, but I could see the mischief in his young eyes; eyes just like Marcos's. As soon as they were out of sight, I knew he would be up to something else terrorizing Marcena or one of the others.

"I think he's gonna be gay," Marcos said. He was joking, but I believed he was serious. He had said it once before.

"It's normal for kids to play with gender inappropriate toys at two and three years old," I told him. I asked, "But if he did end up gay, would you reject him?"

"I'd beat his ass first. I think you got them around Corvell too much," he said.

"So it's not okay for your children to be gay?"

"It's not in our blood to be gay. I ain't got nothing against Corvell or whatever but I ain't cool with that gay shit," he said.

Interesting.

"Let's go out tonight," he suggested.

That was shocking. "Tonight?"

"Yeah," he said. "I gotta meet up with some folks anyway. You might as well come with me."

"Okay," I said without giving it much thought. It wasn't that I was putting the whole Corvell situation aside. I was going to deal with that regardless. I just needed them together.

———————

Before we could go out that night, Marcos got a call. He had to take care of something that for whatever reason I couldn't accompany him. About an hour later I got a call from Corvell. He was upset and crying.

I called Marcos to see where he was and if he still had intentions to go out. He didn't answer my call. I called Corvell back and told him I was coming over to see about him.

When I got to Corvell, I didn't expect to see him beat up so bad.

"What happened?" I asked tending to Corvell's wounds right away. His face was battered badly, and it looked like the work of Marcos.

"I don't know," Corvell cried. "He just went off on me. He was here earlier, and things were fine. He left but said he would be back. I called him, and he didn't answer the phone, so I text him to tell him don't worry about coming back because I was going out."

"So, he showed up and beat the shit out of you?" I asked.

"He's becoming more controlling I guess," Corvell said. "He doesn't want me going out."

"Who is he Corvell?" I wanted him to tell me.

Corvell shook his head. "I can't tell you."

"But I'm your best friend. Why can't you tell me?" I asked, almost desperately.

"Because I just can't," Corvell said.

I stood up, and I asked, "Corvell, I'm gonna ask you something, and I want you to be completely honest with me."

"What?"

"Are you fucking my husband?"

Corvell looked at me with a stunned expression. He frowned as if he didn't want to answer.

I needed to know. "Are you?"

The doorknob to his front door began to turn. Corvell panicked. "Oh shit! Go to my room Nephia!"

"Why?" I asked.

Corvell pushed me towards his bedroom. I ducked inside but didn't shut the door. As soon as Corvell turned his attention back to his door, I heard his voice.

"Why you didn't answer your phone Vell?"

"I didn't hear it," Corvell said. I could detect the nervousness in Corvell's voice as he spoke. "Look, I ain't trying to fight with you anymore."

"I didn't come back over here to fight with you again. You be making me mad with all that whining and shit Vell. I try to spend as much time as I can with you, you know that. I love you, but you always wanna fuck with me tryna find another nigga out there to take my place. I ain't having that."

"I'm not trying to replace you. You know how I feel about you too," Corvell cried. "Baby, I don't want no other nigga but you."

There was silence. I had to hold still because I couldn't blow my cover at this point. When I heard them kissing, I covered my mouth. I couldn't believe this shit!

Well apparently, when I moved, my shadow did too. Thanks a lot, shadow!

"Who's back there?"

Corvell answered quickly, "Nobody."

"Who the fuck is in here Vell?"

"Nobody," Corvell said again. "Baby, c'mon and—"

"Hold the fuck on."

Shit! I couldn't do anything but stand there. I held my breath as two wheat Timbs stood before me. Sheepishly I looked up and smiled. "Hi."

Corvell was right there. "Baby, let me explain!"

I stepped in front of Corvell so that he wouldn't get attacked. "Wait Boogie! Don't get mad. I promise I won't tell a soul."

Boogie looked like his whole world had just come to an end. "Why the fuck y'all playing with me?"

"I wasn't supposed to know," I told him. "I came over here

140

because he was upset." I pointed to Corvell's face and glared at Boogie. "Why you do that to him?"

"Go on Nephia," Boogie said pushing me aside. He got in Corvell's face and threatened, "I'ma fuck yo ass up."

"She won't tell," Corvell tried to tell him. Boogie continued to walk to the front door. He left out slamming the door behind him.

Corvell's shoulders dropped. "He gonna kill me now."

I went to Corvell's living room window and peeked out. Boogie was driving Marcos's Escalade. Where was Marcos?

I turned to a distraught Corvell. "He's not gonna do anything to you. Who all knows about you two?"

"Nobody. No one was supposed to ever know," Corvell said.

"Is he who you've been seeing all these years?"

Corvell nodded.

"If he does anything else to you I'll tell everybody myself."

Corvell shook his head emphatically. "No! Just leave it alone. Doing that will run him away, and that's not what I want."

"So, you'd rather accept what he gives you along with the bruises?"

"If it means I get to be with him," Corvell said pitifully.

"Do you really love him like that Corvell?"

Corvell nodded.

"He's never gonna be able to be with you the way you want. Somebody like Boogie will deny being gay 'til the day he die. And he'd kill himself before letting Marcos and the rest of them know."

"I know that," he said.

"And that's what you want?"

"It's no different from you suffering through Marcos's shit. And why would you think I would fuck Marcos? First of all, I wouldn't do that to you. Second of all, Marcos is too pretty. I like my men a little rough around the edges."

"I assumed because...I saw Marcos's truck here earlier. I was gonna come in to see you, but I was thrown by him being here. But now I know it wasn't him; it was Boogie. However; Marcos left the house over an hour ago in his truck. Where is Marcos?" I wondered.

Corvell cleared his throat with uneasiness. He knew something. I looked over at him, but he tried to avoid eye contact.

"You know where he is don't you?" I asked.

"I have no idea where Marcos is," Corvell said.

"Corvell, don't lie to me. We're in this together," I told him.

"Boogie dropped him off somewhere," he said.

"Where?"

"The hospital."

"What hospital and why?" I asked.

"Uhm...some girl supposed to be...," his voice trailed as he noticed my anger building up. I already knew what he was about to say.

I screamed out in frustration.

"Nephia, it's probably not even his."

"You knew about this?" I asked. The tears came rushing. They were angry tears mixed with the hurt ones. And some of them were caused by Corvell's disloyalty.

"Boogie told me about it. I'm not supposed to know."

"So my husband got some other girl pregnant?"

"He doesn't think it's his though."

"What hospital?" I demanded to know as I gathered my things.

"Don't go up there. You're just gonna make things bad for you."

"He was supposed to be taking me out tonight, but he left so he can attend the birth of another woman's child," I cried. I screamed again. "I'm so sick of this!"

"What are you gonna do?"

"I don't wanna be with him anymore," I said shaking my head. "I'm so done."

"No, you're not," Corvell said. "So just calm down. Go back home and don't say anything."

———

I didn't listen to Corvell. I went home, and I packed the kids and me some clothes.

"Where are you going?" Jovelyn asked.

"We're leaving," I said. "Go pack you some clothes."

Jovelyn was confused. "Where we going?"

"Somewhere other than here," I told her. I went to my mama's room. "C'mon Mama. Hurry up before Marcos gets back."

Lailani was slow poking around. "I'm tired Nephia."

"But we gotta go," I said.

"Why?" Jovelyn asked.

"Are we leaving Daddy?" Marcena asked me.

Yanna started fighting me because she wanted to be put down. "No!"

"You better stop shouting at me," I told her. She stood there with her face scowled up. She was a trip. To be only one she thought she was the boss of everyone.

Bleu and Azul ran around like they had no care in the world.

"Mama and Jovi, grab them," I told them.

Whether they liked it or not, understood or not; I needed to leave and be free of Marcos. After thirty minutes of fussing, I finally had everyone in line. Lailani had Yanna, I had Stormi, and Jovelyn had Raiyne. Marcena held onto either of her brothers' hands and followed behind me.

As we headed out of the front door, Marcos's truck was pulling into the driveway. Not paying him attention I continued with loading the kids in my Tahoe and Jovelyn's Rav4.

Marcos got out of his truck wearing a puzzled expression. "Whoa! What's going on? Where are y'all going this late at night? Why you got the babies out like this Nephia?"

"We're leaving," I told him firmly.

"Leaving?"

"Yeah," I said. I shut the door to the Rav4 and headed back

to my truck.

"What the fuck you talking about?" Marcos asked. He opened the back door to the Rav4. "Y'all get out and take ya ass back in the house."

"No!" I yelled. "We're leaving. I don't want to be here anymore."

Marcos looked at Jovelyn and told her, "Get out and take them back in the house."

"No, you don't. Lock the door and drive!"

Marcos smacked me. "You silly bitch! So you're tryna leave me!"

Lailani got out of my truck and screamed frantically. "No Marcos! The kids!"

"Take them in the house! Now!" His voice roared.

I couldn't see what they were doing because Marcos had walked upon me blocking my view. I was now against my truck waiting for his next move. He slapped me back and forward between his right hand and his left hand.

"Why are you fucking with me! I give you every goddamn thing to make you happy! And now you wanna pull some bullshit like this! Get in the mothafuckin house!"

"No," I said breathlessly.

"No?"

He was enraged. That beautiful fountain in the courtyard was where he drugged me to. He forced my head into the water and held me down. I thought I was gonna die.

He brought me back up. "You ready to go in the mothafuckin house now?"

I couldn't catch my breath to even answer before he was shoving me back in the water. He held me down longer.

"Are you ready now!"

"Yes!" I managed to get out. He never released his hold on my neck. He half pushed half dragged me back in the house. I was thankful that Jovelyn and my mama had acted fast and got the kids out of the way. Although they couldn't see their father beating their mother, I'm sure they heard me that night. Marcos stomped the dog shit out of me. From the front door all the way to our bedroom.

I couldn't even remember half the stuff he had done to me the next morning. All I know was I felt like Tina in *What's Love Got to Do With It* when she had had enough and tried to kill herself.

I laid in my hospital room bed and remained quiet. I didn't even talk to the doctors and nurses.

"She still seems to be in quite a bit of a shock. And with these type of incidents, it's expected," the doctor explained. "Sometimes it takes a while. Just give her some space, and when she's ready, she'll talk. I definitely urge you to continue with counseling once she's discharged. The psychiatrist that assessed her has already set up her first appointment in her office for next week. She says she's showing signs of post-traumatic stress disorder for sure."

The irony of it all! The doctor was talking to the man who had done this to me. Marcos stood off to the side as if he was a concerned husband who happened to come to his wife's aide after being attacked and robbed. That's what he told the authorities and the hospital staff. I wanted to laugh, but the pain from my broken ribs wouldn't let me. My face was so swollen I doubt it could even form a smile.

Beverly waltzed into the room with her usual dramatics. "Oh dear! How are you feeling?"

Marcos looked back at his mother. "Ma, don't bother her."

Beverly sat down on the edge of the bed and caressed my face. She continued to talk to me soothingly with sorrow in her eyes. She whispered, "You've got to stop doing this to yourself, sweetie."

She knew her son had done this to me. She bent down to kiss my forehead. "The less you fight, the better it gets. He loves you. I know he does, but you're gonna make him kill you one day."

I cried silently. There was no hope for me.

Beverly wiped away my tears. "We gotta get you better for my grandbabies. They can't see their mother like this. Would you like for me to stay at the house to help out for a while?"

I nodded.

The doctor left. Marcos walked over to the bed and looked down at me. Usually, after beating me, he showed a little remorse and was apologetic. Not this time. I disgusted him now.

"See the bullshit you put me through," he growled at me. I flinched because I thought he was going to hit me again. "You creating unnecessary medical bills and shit. And as soon as your ass heal, I'ma fuck you up again."

"Marcos, don't be saying stupid shit like that," Beverly chastised.

"She a dumb ass bitch," he said.

"Why don't you go home," she said.

"Nope cause I don't trust her stupid ass," he said. "I'ma be up here until they discharge her."

I continued to cry and sniffle. I made up my mind right then and there that I would take my own life. I wasn't sure when, but I had to do it.

Chapter 11

Taking my life was selfish, so I put that plan on the back burner. I couldn't do that to my children. I took Beverly's advice and just shut up.

By the time I went home after that incident, Marcos had calmed down. He kept his distance. However in January when my twenty-first birthday came around, he whisked me away on a tour of several Caribbean islands for about three weeks. We didn't travel alone. It was a group of us, and I must say it was one of my best birthday celebrations.

I had Bridgette, Nikki, Corvell, and Chrissy all with me and we had a fabulous time. And despite the wedge between Marcos and me, we even enjoyed one another. He catered to me a lot. He even kept his wandering eyes from roaming during that time. It was all about me.

I didn't even want the vacation to end. Oh! And I got a kick out of watching Corvell and Boogie act as if they disgusted one another. I even covered for them so they could sneak off and enjoy some alone time on the islands. Their secret was safe with me. I was just worried about how Boogie was going to handle when the secret came out. But I was happy for Corvell because since I knew, Boogie hadn't been abusive with Corvell anymore.

And that girl that supposedly was pregnant by Marcos admitted that Marcos was not the father. So maybe I got my ass kicked for nothing. He never knew that's why I did what I did. Corvell found out through Boogie that the baby ended up not being Marcos's. But as the years passed, there was always a girl claiming to be carrying Marcos's baby.

Like now. This white bitch Terra was determined to take Marcos away from me. She just didn't know, I wanted her to, but he wasn't giving his family up for her. She and I would argue over the phone because she loved fucking with me. All she was doing was making herself less desirable for Marcos. I wouldn't argue or make a big deal out of it. I would simply tell Marcos, "Terra still calling me. Can you ask her to at least not call after ten."

Marcos wouldn't say anything, but I would hear through the grapevine that her pale white skin had been turned a few shades of purple and blue.

"He don't even want you anymore," Terra was saying to me.

"He don't?" I said sarcastically. "So what makes you think after all these years he's gonna leave me to be with you?"

"He basically done left you already," she pointed out. "Where he be at?"

This was one of those dumb white girls that thought they were black. I often wondered where Marcos find some of these girls. Terra was actually an employee of his. She worked one of his nightclubs or so that's what I had been told. Marcos also had a strip club that he didn't think I knew about. I thought that's where she came from.

"I don't know. Tell me where he *be at*?" I asked mocking her.

"With me and our daughter. He done put us in a four bedroom house and everything," she boasted.

Normally the things she would say to me wouldn't bother me, but when she mentioned "our daughter" she had pushed the right buttons.

She laughed. "Oh yeah, we got a daughter. Why ain't none of your little friends tell you that since they keep you informed about everything else?"

"What do you want Terra?" I asked angrily. "You want me to know all of this for what reason? You want me to leave Marcos? Hell, I've been trying for years. You want him to leave me and have him all to yourself? Take him! But guess what? He won't fucking go!"

"Whatever Nephia," she said blowing out a frustrated breath. "He won't divorce you because he know you'll take everything from him."

I laughed. "That's what he tells you huh? I don't want anything. The only thing I want is my freedom from him. If you want him and the headache that goes along with him, you can have him. Shit, I heard the nigga beating on you too. That's what you want?"

"He don't do half the shit he do to you to me."

"Oh and that's cool?" I shook my head and couldn't help but laugh. "I tell you what. You and I both can confront him together and ask him what he wants. Where is he?"

She didn't say anything.

"Terra, I'm so serious right now because I'm tired of this," I said trying to hold back tears. "If you can take him off my hands I will be forever grateful and indebted to you because I swear I hate him. You can have him."

"He should be home by nine," she told me.

Wow. I knew he had other places he laid his head but hearing another woman comfortably calling her home his home was a big dose of reality.

I got Terra's address and headed over to her house and waited for Marcos to show up. While waiting, she filled me in on their plans of being together. She was a pretty white girl with strawberry blonde hair. She was a little older than I was. She had a nice body for a white girl; you know the kind that looked good in a pair of thongs, but she really didn't have an ass.

But what made all of this tough for me was the two-year-old girl. She looked just like Marcos, Marcena, and Yanna. The only difference was her hair was a dusty auburn unlike all of our ink black hair.

I sat in the den patiently when Marcos walked through the door that led to the garage. He didn't even notice me.

"Baby!" he called out.

Brittani, the two-year-old ran up to him with a smile and reached for him. Marcos lifted her up in his arms and kissed her. "Hey, Daddy's baby. Where your mama at? Terra, what you cook?"

Terra looked at me then focused her eyes on the den's entryway. "I'm in here Marcos."

"You ain't cooked shit?" Marcos asked as he entered the den carrying Brittani.

Terra looked over at me. Marcos turned in my direction. At first, he seemed completely stuck and caught off guard.

I stood up clutching my purse close to me. I sighed feeling defeated. I wanted to get rid of him anyway. It's what I wanted, but I always felt like I was losing. I plastered a sincere smile on my face and said, "Your second home is nice. And your little girl is beautiful. She probably should meet her brothers and sisters one day. I'll let myself out. Y'all enjoy your evening."

I headed towards the living room to exit out of the front door.

"Nephia!"

Marcos was calling after me, but I had no reason to stop to hear what he had to say. Because I didn't want him noticing my vehicle outside of the house, I had parked down the street some ways. I continued my journey to my car.

"Let me explain," Marcos said grabbing me by the arm.

I didn't want to fight with him. I turned to him. "Go ahead."

"She ain't shit to me."

"That ain't what I just saw Marcos. I mean, they *are* your family. And you can't deny lil Brittani. She looks just like Yanna," I said. Then my shoulders dropped, and I begged him. "Just let me go. You can be happy with her. You don't even love me anymore. There's no use in you sticking around just for the sake of appearances. I mean, Brittani is your flesh and blood. How fair is it to her that you abandon her like that?"

"I don't want Terra though," he explained. "I'm just there for Brittani. I would have told you about her a long time ago, but I didn't know how you would feel about it. If you can accept her Nephia, we can make this work. Baby, I'm not letting you go anywhere. I love you, and I want our family to stay together. Do you understand me?"

"Marcos," I said as I tried to search for more words.

He took my face in his hands. "Please Nephia. I love you, and I promise I won't put you through any more bullshit. Just tell me now that we can get through this and I'll go back in there and tell her what the deal is."

I didn't know what to tell him. "Marcos, do whatever you think you need to do. I gotta get back—"

"No Nephia!" he said through gritted teeth. His hold on my face got tighter. "Tell me!"

"Tell you what?" I asked.

"That we're gonna get through this and that you love me."

I think he was high. For safety reasons, I said, "I love you and if you wanna work through this then we can. Go talk to her and put your daughter to bed, Marcos."

He kissed me. "Thank you, baby."

I knew this was the most inappropriate thought, but I knew that I wasn't getting my ass beat that night; Terra was.

I don't know what happened that night, but for almost a year I got somewhat of a loving husband out of the deal. Brittani came over regularly. Marcos was coming home every night. He didn't beat on me either. I mean he would get a little physical like squeezing my hand or my face when he was angered by something. Hell, we even had another baby. This was a boy. After Remi, I convinced Marcos to let me get fixed. I didn't think my body could take another pregnancy. So that's where it stopped. We had seven kids together, and he had Brittani outside of the marriage.

Gradually things returned to "normal." I knew it wouldn't last long. Marcos had left for a few weeks on business. I found out that he had taken Terra on a nice little vacation while I was taking care of Brittani. I didn't take any of my frustrations out on Brittani. She couldn't help who her parents were.

While Marcos was away, I ran into Kendall. I hadn't seen him much after high school. Last I had heard he had moved to Baltimore. That was a few years ago. When I saw him at Bailey's, he was with a few other friends I hadn't seen since high school. The little reunion was a nice one.

"Wow Nephia," Thomas said with awe. "Every time I see you it looks like time is reversing for you. You look younger the older you get."

"Oh hush boy," I told him playfully.

Kendall was looking at me with the same adoration he used to look at me with back in high school.

"Will you stop?" I whispered to him.

"I can't help it," he smiled. "Tommy's right though. You don't seem to be aging at all."

"I guess it's in my genes," I said.

Corvell walked up to me and said, "I'm catching a ride with my brother since he's going in the same direction."

"Are you sure?" I asked.

"Yeah," he said. He grinned down at Kendall. "Besides, it look like y'all could do some catching up."

"There you go," I laughed. "Bye Corvell."

"See y'all," he said before walking away.

Kendall looked back at me. "Do you have to hurry home?"

"No, not really. This my night away," I said.

"Good," he said. "You wanna get out of here and go somewhere a little quieter?"

"Sure, why not," I said.

We ended up going back to his place. Kendall had pursued a college degree in engineering and had obtained a great paying job as one of the senior engineers over at the US Tobacco plant. I learned that he had been living in the Antioch area for about a year. With him living in Antioch, it was understandable why he and I hadn't run into each other much sooner.

Kendall had a son but had never married. He informed me that he and the mother got along fine, but both mutually agreed that they were not made for each other. He said they took turns caring for their son. It was obvious because his second bedroom was definitely a little boy's room. I could tell that his son spent quite a bit of time at Kendall's place.

"I'm not really seeing anybody exclusively at the moment," Kendall was telling me. "How about you?"

"Oh I'm still with Marcos," I said.

Kendall's eyes landed on my bare left hand. He must have assumed I was divorced.

"I took it off," I said.

"Why are you still with him?" Kendall asked.

I shrugged.

He walked to his kitchen, and there was an obvious flaw in his gait. I felt so bad because it was my fault that he ended up injured.

"Do you want anything to drink?" he asked.

"What do you have?"

"Coke, Mt. Dew, wine, Heineken, and some vodka," he chuckled.

"Wow, you have a variety there," I joked. "You got some cranberry juice?"

"Actually, I do. Let me guess, you're a cran and vodka girl?"

I smiled, "I am."

"Coming right up."

We got comfortable on the sofa and talked and talked and talked. Besides talking to Corvell, I hadn't had a decent conversation with a man in a long time. And it didn't hurt that there was growing sexual tension between us either.

"I wish I had entered your life before he did," Kendall said. He brushed my hair back from my face.

"I wish you had to. I know I would be a lot happier."

"I'm here for you Nephia. Know that."

I nodded.

He lifted my face by my chin so that we could lock gazes. He said, "I mean it."

"I know."

His face came closer to mine, and we kissed. It was a soft sensual kiss that did more to me than I expected it to. We pulled back and looked at each other to make sure this was what we wanted to go forward with. I wanted it if he wanted it. I had no objections.

Kendall didn't waste much time getting to what he wanted either. He tugged my pants and panties down. I helped him ease them off of me completely. He pushed me back on the sofa and made himself comfortable in between my legs. He was face to face with my love box. He kissed down my thighs

157

as he widened my legs apart. With my freshly shaven pussy in his face and my hooded clitoris staring him back in the face, Kendall gently rubbed it in a circular motion and watched me squirm a little bit. He then lowered his head down to mimic his finger with his tongue.

"Kendall...," I gasped.

"Hmm?" he hummed as he continued to lick on me. He teased my clit with his stiffened tongue and started moving it rapidly.

"Oh!" I cried out.

He eased a finger inside me and whispered, "It taste better than I imagined." As he stirred my juices, he continued to lap every bit of it up.

"Can I have you Nephia?"

"Yes!"

He removed his finger from me and stood up. He reached for me and helped me to my feet. I caught a glimpse of the missile poking through the front of his pants. I needed to feel him inside me.

Kendall picked me up and threw me over his shoulder. I yelped and giggled as he carried me to his bedroom. He gently laid me on his bed and finished undressing me. He took his time as he admired every inch of my naked body. I knew he was impressed. For a woman to have given birth to seven kids, my body was still in better shape than the average eighteen-year-old. I had stress to thank for that. Besides the stretch marks under my navel and around my hips, a person couldn't tell I was even a mother.

Kendall undressed, and I was just as impressed with him.

Despite not going off to be a professional football player, Kendall's body was still very much in shape. And his dick was just as impressive.

He ordered me on all fours with my ass up and my shoulders touching the bed. The next sensations I felt was Kendall eating me from behind. He ran his tongue from my ass all the way up to my stiff clit. I was trembling and moaning loudly. I know the neighbors had to hear me. Kendall tried to lick all of my nectar as my juices ran down my thighs.

"Ah! Kendall," my voice quivered. "Baby, I'm about to cum..."

He beat my clit with his tongue and didn't let up even as I screamed out in orgasm. With my ass still in the air, he swiftly positioned himself behind me and entered my gripping wet walls. He groaned, "Damn girl!"

"Baby," I cried as he began stroking me hard and fast.

"Hmm?"

I gripped the cover in my hands and tried to stifle my whimpers by biting a mouthful of his comforter.

"Oh Nephia, you feel so damn good!" he cried out as he dug deeper.

"Don't stop!" I begged. I needed this. I loved the way he pounded me relentlessly. He fucked me like he had to prove something. Perhaps he wanted me to always remember him. Or better yet, make me want to come back for more. Regardless, Kendall put it on me.

We fucked all night. I was so tired, so spent that I didn't leave his house until the following afternoon. When I left, I promised that he would hear from me soon.

When Marcos had returned from his secret vacation a week later, I was just as rejuvenated as he was. Hell, I had crept over to Kendall's and let him get me right a few more times. I wasn't thinking about Marcos's ass.

"Did you miss me?" Marcos asked playfully.

I looked up from the magazine I was reading. I said as an observation, "Oh, you have a tan." I went back to reading the magazine.

"That's all you gotta say? You haven't seen your husband in almost a month, and that's all you gotta say."

I gave it some thought. "Yeah."

Marcos frowned. "What's up with you Nephia?"

"Nothing," I said.

"Well damn, I miss you," he said. He moved closer to me.

I inched away from him. "I'm good."

"You didn't miss me?"

I shook my head. "I actually enjoyed you being away. We need our space."

He knew I was being facetious now because even when he was home, Marcos made sure we had enough space by staying with other women.

Marcos grabbed a handful of my ass and squeezed. "I miss this. Can I have some of this?"

I removed his hand from me. "I'm on my period."

"So," he said.

"I am not having sex on my period."

160

"It ain't like you ain't never did it before," he said with a laugh.

"Yeah, and I didn't like it."

Marcos kissed my cheek. "Let me go hang with the kids for a minute."

"Yeah," I said nonchalantly.

I don't think he liked the way I was behaving. He didn't walk away from me immediately. He hesitated and stared at me for a minute. I looked up at him and smiled. He went ahead with his business.

I messed up when I let my guard down later that night. I had taken a shower and went to bed as I always did. Marcos came into the room and tended to his own shower in his own bathroom.

I was half sleeping when he came jumping on me. He had me pinned down, and I was looking at him like he was crazy.

"Why you lie to me?"

"What are you talking about?" I asked.

"You're not on your period!"

"Can you get off of me?"

With one hand he kept my hands pinned above my head. With the other hand, he reached under my nightshirt and snatched my panties down.

"Where's your period, Nephia?"

"I just went off," I lied.

"You don't want me fucking you Nephia?"

"Aren't you getting enough elsewhere Marcos?" I shot

back.

"Don't get smart with me," he said. He pinched the lips of my pussy hard.

I winced in pain. "Don't start this shit Marcos."

"Why did you lie to me?"

"I didn't. I just saw that I was off."

He released my arms so that he could tug my panties down my legs. He tossed them aside. He inserted a finger inside me and kept his eyes on me. He removed his finger and brought it up to his nose. He sniffed it then stuck it in his mouth.

I waited to see what his analysis was going to come back with. I guess I was good because he spread my legs apart so that he could continue to taste me. Shit, I let him. It was feeling too good to stop him.

The whole time he was down there I imagined that it was Kendall. I would have rather it been Kendall.

Marcos got more aggressive with me than he usually did. I liked it, but I wasn't sure if he was feeling a certain way or if he was mad.

I smiled to myself because I felt like I was just as equal as he was now. I had slept with someone else too.

Chapter 12

Two things happened in the year 2010. My father, Ben Blackwood showed up out of nowhere. It was awkward at first. Lailani was the only one that was super thrilled about the family reunion.

I met my older brother, Ben Jr. and my older sister Ashli. I didn't really like them. They acted rather snooty. I don't think they were expecting for us to be living as good as we were. When I invited them to the house, they all were impressed. I don't know if it was our wealth that made knowing me more appealing, but Ben maintained communication with me and tried to be active in his grandchildren's lives. I appreciated it and wouldn't complain.

Ashli wanted my husband though. I had to watch her.

The second thing that happened right before our ten-year class reunion was Boogie being killed. Some young boys robbed him and shot him fatally. Marcos, Gogo, and Quan took it very hard. But my heart went out to Corvell.

Boogie and Corvell had been secret lovers for ten years. No one knew about it except me.

"How can I go to his funeral and pretend like I'm not dying inside!" Corvell cried to me.

I held him. "I don't know. Maybe, you shouldn't go."

"I gotta go," he said.

"Well I'll be there, and we'll get through it together," I assured him.

"I don't think I can do it."

"Then stay home."

"I gotta go."

"Okay." I got quiet.

Corvell started sobbing again. "I'm not gonna be able to make it."

"I know so that's why you should stay home."

"I gotta go."

I rubbed his back soothingly. "Are you ready?"

"No!"

I looked at the time. I was supposed to have accompanied Marcos to the funeral, but I had to be here for Corvell. "The funeral starts in about thirty minutes."

Corvell lifted his head from my bosom and took a deep breath. "Okay. I think I can do this."

"Are you sure?"

He nodded. "Let me get my face together."

My cell phone rang. It was Nikki. "Hey."

"Are y'all on the way to the funeral?"

"Yeah, you know how Corvell is. He takes forever," I said.

"Okay, I'm just gonna wait in the parking lot until I see y'all," she said. "I just saw Boogie's baby mama going in. Girl, she looks so pitiful."

Not as pitiful as Corvell, I wanted to say.

"I bet," I said. "I'll be there though."

"Okay," she said and ended the call.

Corvell came back into the living room more composed,

but his eyes were still red and puffy.

I reached out for him to take my hand. "We'll get through this."

He offered me an unsure smile but took my hand.

Now, I know the funeral wasn't about no one else except for Johnathan "Boogie" Lawrence; however, I did not appreciate Terra or Draya being there. I heard Draya and Marcos had been hooking up. But what made her think she should be sitting beside my husband? Hell, even Terra wasn't feeling that.

I looked at Corvell and whispered to him, "Do you want to go up there?"

"Only if you come with me," he told me.

Corvell held onto my hand so hard I thought he was going to break it. He was so anxious and so nervous. I felt really bad for him.

We stood before Boogie's open casket. I was on one side of Corvell and Nikki was on the other side of him. She had no idea what was going on, but Corvell was fucking my hand up!

"Are you okay?" I asked.

Corvell just stared at Boogie's body. I said a quick prayer and asked God to, please let Corvell keep it together. Letting the world know that Boogie was gay at his funeral was not the best timing at all.

Corvell whispered, "He wouldn't have wanted to wear this."

Nikki said, "Huh?"

I giggled. Corvell was getting mad. "He didn't even like

wearing suits. This don't even look like him. But it is him. Look at his lil baby dreads."

Nikki was really confused. "What?"

I had to stifle my laughs and at the same time pull Corvell away so that the people behind us could view the body.

"I love you J Boogie," Corvell said under his breath.

Nikki stood there looking after me and Corvell as we walked away. She looked back at Boogie, and I could see the wheels beginning to turn.

I was so consumed with Corvell and trying to keep him acting right, I had forgotten about Marcos and his disrespectful women.

At Boogie's mother's house during the repast, I was pleasantly surprised to see Kendall there. He was there with a few guys and was paying their respects to Boogie's brother and family.

"Hey Nephia," Kendall said. His eyes were saying something else.

I smile, "Hey, how are you, Kendall?"

"I'm good," he said. No, he wasn't. He wanted me bad. I could see it in his eyes. For four years he and I had maintained our secret affair. We didn't overdo it so we wouldn't get caught up. It was every once in a while where we would allocate some special time just to enjoy each other and get away from the realities of our own lives.

I had to give it to him though. Kendall was not afraid of Marcos's presence. And whenever he bumped into Marcos, he always politely spoke and kept it moving.

"I'll see you around," I told him. That meant I would be

calling him soon.

When I turned away from him, Marcos was burning a hole in me from across the room. He wasn't too happy. I smiled his way and went to look for Corvell. I found him in Ms. Lawrence's living room looking at old photos of a young Boogie.

"How are you feeling?" I asked.

"I'm okay," he said. He looked around, and his eyes landed on Boogie's baby mama. "I think she had him killed."

"Corvell! You can't be saying shit like that," I told him.

"I'm so serious. He was telling me they hadn't been getting along. Then she threatened to tell everybody that he was down low," he told me in a hushed tone.

"What do you mean?" I asked.

"Oh, she found out that he was talking to a dude. She just didn't know who it was."

"How this happen?"

Corvell side eyed me. "Oh, you would have known if you hadn't been sneaking dick on the side."

I placed my fingers up to my mouth to make him shut up.

"Well, why you were busy swallowing another nigga's babies—"

"Corvell!"

He snickered, "Okay! Apparently, she had been going through his phone and came across our texts. She thought I was another female he was messing around with. She called me from his phone, and I thought it was him calling, so I answered like I always did when he called. I said, 'My Boogie must be missing this ass.' All I got was silence. So I was like, 'J Boogie?'. Then she was like, 'This ain't Boogie. Who is this?'. I hung up cause I didn't know what to say."

This was good. "So, what happened?"

"She called me back. I didn't answer. She tried to call me back from another number. I still didn't answer. Then she started texting me a bunch of crazy shit. A couple of days later, Boogie came over and told me what happened and how they had a really big fight. I asked him if he wanted to chill since she suspected. He told me fuck her. A few days later..." his voice trailed.

My smile disappeared too. She did appear a little suspect, and her grief seemed force.

"Excuse me?"

Corvell and I both turned around to see Ms. Lawrence standing there. She looked at Corvell and asked, "Can I talk to you in private?"

Corvell frowned with suspicion and looked at me. I looked back at him.

"Why?" Corvell asked.

"You're Corvell Armstrong right?" she asked.

Corvell nodded.

She smiled. "Then you're who I need to talk to."

Corvell grabbed my hand and started squeezing again.

Ms. Lawrence looked over at me.

Corvell said, "Whatever you need to say you can say in front of her."

Ms. Lawrence said, "Okay. I knew about you. Johnathan

confided in me earlier this year. As quiet as its kept, I already knew my son's tendencies. But I want you to have these."

She produced a clasped orange envelope. She put it in Corvell's hands. She gave Corvell a pat on his shoulder and smiled at him. "You take care son."

Corvell and I both were stunned. He looked around to see who was paying attention to the exchange that had just taken place. A few nosy people were staring at us. I pulled Corvell along, and we headed out of the house through the front door. We went all the way down to where I parked my car and hopped in. We were both excited acting like Shug and Celie from *The Color Purple* when they found those letters. He went to open the envelope until we both were startled by pounding on the window.

"Let me in!" It was Nikki.

I unlocked the door for her, and she jumped in the back. Leaning in between our seats she asked, "What the hell is going on? Everybody wanna know what Boogie mama gave y'all."

I locked the doors. "We don't know."

Corvell opened the envelope and reached inside. It was Boogie's cherished chains he used to wear around his neck, a key, a check with about five digits on it, a picture of him and Corvell that looked like just two guy friends hanging out, and a letter. I took the picture from Corvell and studied it. I recognized it as one of the photos they had taken during our trip to the islands. I smiled because I remembered how silly they were being.

Nikki didn't say anything. She just looked at everything sadly.

When we heard Corvell sucking up snot, she and I both turned our attention to him. He was bawling again. Whatever was in that letter was very personal. Corvell clutched the letter to his chest and just cried.

"Who was it from?" I asked. He couldn't reply. I asked, "Was it a letter from Boogie?"

Corvell nodded.

Nikki started crying. "This is more heart wrenching than I thought. Y'all were gay lovers and were in love for real!"

I laughed, but my laughter faded into sobs too. All three of us sat in my car crying like we were crazy.

"Oh shit!" Nikki exclaimed through her tears. She grabbed everything from Corvell and started stuffing it back in the envelope.

I looked up and saw Marcos, Gogo, and Quan headed right for us.

Before Marcos could even demand that I roll the window down, I had it coming down.

"What the fuck going on?" he asked.

"Nothing," I answered.

He looked at me, then over at Corvell and then at Nikki. We all looked a mess.

"What was that Boogie mama gave y'all?" Marcos asked.

Nikki clutched the envelope to her. "None of your business. It's between me and Boogie."

"So you and Boogie had some secret thing going on?" Quan asked.

"Like I said, it's none of your business," Nikki said with

defiance. "If he wanted y'all to know he would have told you while he was living. He's gone now. So if you don't mind, can I grieve in peace?"

"Excuse me," Quan said as he backed away from the car.

"So all y'all mothafuckas sitting in the car crying together?" Marcos asked.

All three of us nodded our heads.

"Y'all some mothafuckin' goofballs," Gogo said shaking his head.

"Takes one to know one," I countered playfully.

Gogo walked away with Quan.

Marcos said, "After you finish being stupid with your girlfriends, bring your ass back in the house."

"Okay," I said. We watched them walk away in silence.

Corvell said, "Thanks y'all."

"No problem," I said. I leaned over and gave him a hug.

"Hey I want some hug action," Nikki said as she wrapped her arms around us.

Sometimes I think if it weren't for Nikki and Corvell, I would have lost my mind a long time ago. And even with my messed-up situation, I knew I was the same support for them. We had a bond that could not be broken.

———————

"Nephia?"

"Hmm?"

"You know you can't go to sleep baby."

171

I groaned. "Just for a little while."

Kendall kissed me on my nose. "No, because I will enjoy the feel of you next to me and I won't wake up in time."

"Why don't you call Marcos for me and just tell him I'm not coming home," I joked.

"You know I have no problem with that," Kendall said.

I opened my eyes and stared up into Kendall's face. "You're ready for me to leave him aren't you?"

"You already know the answer to that," he said. He kissed me on the lips. "But this isn't about pressuring you to make any moves."

"I know," I sighed. "I keep thinking about how we could be putting all of this behind us and being happy together."

"Well I'm ready whenever you are," he said.

"I think I'm ready," I said quietly.

"You don't need to talk to him about this alone Nephia," Kendall said. "When you're sure you're ready to make that move let me know so that I can be right there with you."

"How come you're not scared of Marcos?"

"He's nothing to be scared of. He's a coward and would never fight a man like me one on one with no weapons. He knows I'd kick his ass. Have you noticed he ain't never really jumped bad with me unless he get a group of his flunkies to gang me like they did years ago?"

Kendall had a point. This was interesting because Marcos had never really challenged Kendall before. Maybe there was some truth to what Kendall was saying.

"You need to be going because I don't want him putting

his hands on you," Kendall said.

I reluctantly got out of his bed and headed to his bathroom. I took a quick shower. When I stepped out of the bathroom, Kendall had slipped his sweatpants back on. Since he hadn't showered, I had to avoid coming in close contact with him. Marcos would sniff his scent on me with no problem.

"I'll talk to you later," I said. We leaned toward each other and pecked on the lips.

"I love you Nephia. And be careful," he told me.

"I love you too," I told him.

Once I got in my car, I called Corvell.

"Hey hoe!" he chimed.

"Whatever. Has he called looking for me?"

"Nope."

"Good. I doubt he's looking for me anyway. I think they were having something down at the club anyway." I said.

"Well call me when you make it in the house," Corvell said.

"I will," I said.

"Love ya hoe!" he laughed.

I ended the call with him. It had been months since Boogie died, but Corvell was recuperating from it very well. I think it had a lot to do with the letter Boogie had written him. Boogie didn't know he would be dead when he was writing the letter. It was just something that he wrote Corvell one day and never gave it to him. It was a letter telling Corvell all of the things he wished he could do and would do one day and the things he wished he could change and take back just to make Corvell happy one day. He had shown his mother the letter when he confessed to her his feelings for another man. She thought it was too beautiful for Boogie to shred it, so she kept it.

I was envious of Corvell because even though Boogie started off with his faults, he had straightened up and truly loved Corvell. I wished Marcos would see me like that one day.

Chapter 13

Although Kendall and I had talked about making a move, I couldn't quite go through with it. I loved Kendall, but I wanted Marcos to love me more. This caused a rift between me and Kendall because I had pulled back drastically.

It was 2012 now. I wasn't being fair to Kendall, but I still wanted him waiting in the wings for me especially to love me and make me feel special after Marcos would tear me down. In a way, I had developed this unhealthy back and forward dependency on both men.

"I'm so sick of this shit Nephia!" Kendall shouted.

He rarely got loud with me, but he was losing his patience.

"I know, and I'm sorry," I told him. "I just can't leave right now."

"It ain't like he's treating you any better," he pointed out. "I could see if the nigga was coming home and taking you places with him. He's not! Every time I see him out, and about he got some new bitch on his arm. He's parading these desperate ass bitches around while you sit at home playing good wife and mother to all of his kids. Hell, you're even playing mama to his baby mama's child so they can fuck all night! What the fuck!"

"Ssh," I closed my eyes. "I know, but it's not that easy Kendall."

"Easy? We've been seeing each other for six years now! I've been waiting for you to make a move for six years! I can't wait forever, baby."

I walked upon him. "I know, I know. I'll try to come up with something."

Kendall wrapped his arms around me. He chuckled, "You're drunk, you know that?"

"I know, I know," I whispered.

"I can't let you drive home yet," he said.

"But I gotta get back home," I told him.

"Not like this. Call Corvell and Nikki and tell them you're at one of their houses," he said. "I'm not letting you leave like this. I told you to slow down anyway."

"I know, I know," I repeated. My eyes closed before I crawled back in his bed. I was still naked and hadn't bothered to wash up. I did drink too much. What was I thinking?

"You gotta call Corvell first baby."

"You do it," I told him as I felt myself drifting off to sleep.

It was the middle of the night when I woke up in a panic. I prayed Marcos was still out and hadn't decided to come back home of all nights.

I awakened Kendall as I frantically looked for my clothes.

"Baby, what are you doing?"

"I gotta go!" I whispered yelled. "Why did you let me sleep so late?"

"Because you had drunk too much. C'mon and lay back down. You're okay," he said.

"No, you don't understand. I need to be gone Kendall," I said. "Where's my damn panties?"

"Baby, get back in the bed," Kendall groaned. "You're

spending the night over Corvell's. He and I already discussed it. And Jovelyn said that your mama said Marcos isn't even home anyway. You're good. So go ahead and get in this damn bed with me."

"So you took care of everything for me?" I asked.

"Yes," he said tiredly.

"Okay," I said. Against my better judgment, I crawled back in bed with him.

The following morning I didn't care how much he tried to convince me to stay, I had to leave.

When I charged up my phone and finally powered it back on, I started getting a lot of notifications back to back. It was everything I had missed overnight when my phone must have died. While trying to drive, I looked down at my screen and noticed I had several missed calls, several voicemail messages, and several unread text messages. I immediately thought something bad had happened to one of the kids.

Before I could call home, my phone was ringing. I answered it, "Hello?"

"Where are you? Oh my God!" Corvell exclaimed. He didn't sound good at all.

"What is it?"

"I didn't know what to tell him!"

"What!"

"Marcos!"

"What do you mean?"

"Hold on. Nikki's calling me back," he said.

"No! She can wait. What's going on?"

"She probably calling me back cause she just got off the phone with his ass!"

"Why is he calling her?"

"Hold on!"

Shit! I was getting anxious. I needed to know what was going on before I took my ass home.

"Nephia?"

"What's going on Corvell?"

"Marcos was looking for you? I didn't know what I was supposed to tell him. He hung up with me then called Nikki. We hadn't had time to talk to each other and get our lie together. He caught us up."

"But I thought you knew to tell him I was spending the night with you!" I was ready to cry.

"I didn't know that! You never told me that."

"But I thought you talked to Kendall last night."

"I ain't talked to no damn Kendall last night."

"But he said he talked to you and y'all had it all straight."

"He didn't talk to me. Maybe he meant Nikki, but then that wouldn't make sense cause she didn't know what to tell Marcos either."

My heart sank as I realized what Kendall did. "That mothafucka! Oh my God Corvell! Marcos is finna kick my ass. I didn't go home last night. I was with Kendall all night."

"Bitch, don't go home! You better take yo ass straight to Mexico and hide out some damn where! This nigga is heated!"

"Please don't tell me that," I groaned.

"Maybe you could tell him you were with that ugly sister of yours," Corvell suggested.

"Who Ashli?"

"Yeah, that bitch."

"He knows I don't like her. Hell, he probably called her too."

"Well look, you don't need to go home although I don't think he was even at home when he called."

"Why is that?"

"Because it sounded like he was driving."

"Okay. Well, maybe he doesn't even know I stayed out all night. He probably just wondering where I am now. But he's still gonna wonder why you and Nikki were trying to lie," I said feeling a little better.

"Fuck! Shit, I don't know what to tell ya," Corvell said.

My line beeped. It was Marcos. "It's him. I'll call you back."

I switched lines. "Hello?"

"Where are you?" Marcos asked.

"I'm on my way home," I told him casually. "Where are you?"

"On my way home too. Where are you coming from?" I didn't like how calm he was talking. Something was up.

"I got up to go to the market this morning," I lied.

He laughed. "You went to the market?"

I laughed nervously. "Yeah. Why is that funny?"

"When the last time you walked your ass around at the market baby?"

"I go with Ada and Mama sometimes," I told him.

"Well did you get anything?"

"Nah," I answered. "I couldn't really look around like I wanted to because my stomach started hurting. That's why I'm on my way home."

"Oh."

"So where are you coming from?" I asked.

"I just left IHOP," he said.

"So you've already had breakfast?"

"Yeah, I was calling you to see if you wanted anything but the phone kept going to voicemail. I got worried and called the house. They said you weren't there. So I called Corvell and Nikki. You got some goofy ass friends. I don't know what the hell they were trying to tell me, but they couldn't keep their lies straight."

"Huh?" I chuckled feigning confusion.

"Yeah, I guess they thought I was mad or something and they were trying to cover for you. I could tell they were lying but they silly like that."

"I don't even know why they did that," I said. My nerves were settling already.

"I don't either," he said. "But I'll see you in a minute. How far away from home are you?"

Damn. I was further away than I should have been if I was just going to the market. I lied, "I uhm...not that far from the neighborhood."

"Okay. I'll see you in a minute."

And he hung up. I let out a big sigh of relief.

I was so glad I had gotten to the house before he did too. It allowed me time to change clothes. I was coming out of my closet when Marcos was walking in the bedroom. Two things stopped me in my tracks. The first thing was Marcos was not dressed as if he had just left a club and hit IHOP up for breakfast.

This nigga was wearing black!

Marcos doesn't wear anything except for white clothes! He may wear denim jeans or colored jeans, but he always wore white along with it. To see him in all black was rare. I don't think I've ever had the pleasure of seeing him in black.

The second thing that caused me to pause was that his expression did not match the calm tone he was using with me over the phone. His eyes were red and swollen like he had been crying. He stared at me with this fire in his eyes that had the look of a man betrayed and hurt.

"What's wrong?" I asked. My eyes landed on his gloved hands. Why was he wearing gloves?

"C'mere baby," he told me. He reached out to me.

I wasn't sure if it was safe.

"Nephia, please come to me," he said.

"Marcos," I said cautiously. "You're scaring me. What's wrong?"

He dropped to his knees, and he started to cry. "Please baby, just come to me."

I went to him. He wrapped his arms around my waist and buried his face in my stomach. He was holding me so tight that if it were possible, we would have become one.

"It's okay," I soothed him.

"I love you so much. You mean the world to me Nephia," he cried.

"Okay," I said.

"Baby, don't ever leave me!"

"I won't," I said. His grip on me was so strong it was starting to pull me down.

"You belong to me! Do you love me?"

"Yeah, I love you."

"And you won't ever leave me?"

"No—" I was saying but that "No" turned into a scream as I felt his teeth clench down hard on my stomach. Like the death grip of a pit bull, he wouldn't let me go. I had to hit him and pull away at the same time.

I didn't have time to ask questions. I immediately went into flee mode. Before I could get away from him,, he had grabbed me by my leg and tripped me causing me to fall hard on my ass. To slow me down he struck me in my face one good time to daze me.

"Get up!" He yelled at me. He was now standing over me.

I crossed my arms over me to protect me from another blow.

"Get the fuck up!" he demanded.

"Okay! Please don't hit me," I begged.

"Bitch, I'll do whatever the fuck I want to when it comes to your lying hoe ass!" Instead of hitting me he stomped my thigh.

I cried out in pain.

He slapped me and spat, "I said get the fuck up!"

"What did I do?" I cried.

"I'm about to show you. Get up!"

I managed to get up. Marcos removed his phone from his pocket. He started playing a video. He put it in my face. "Ain't this you?"

I needed God to take me at that moment. I would have rather been struck by lightning than standing before Marcos after I glanced at that video. Before I could even react to it, Marcos had slammed the phone so hard in my face it sent me flying sideways.

"You watch this shit!" he said putting the phone back in my face.

It was me and Kendall. It started with him recording me in a half stupor half alert state. He was asking me questions, and I was answering them. I was smiling with my eyes closed. I was naked. He hovered the camera over my body and zoomed in on my pussy. He played in it and showed me responding to him. He asked me if I liked it. I moaned. Then the camera went out of focus, but you could hear what was taking place. I was moaning loud, and you could hear Kendall slurping on my pussy. Then he picked the phone back up and held it over my pussy as he pushed his dick inside me. The camera captured inch by inch of his dick disappearing inside me. He started pumping faster and breathing harder. My eyes flew open and called out his name.

Marcos bashed the phone upside my head several times. I just knew I was about to pass out.

"Bitch, you bet not pass out on me! You staying up for all this shit!"

Weakened and barely able to focus, I said, "I'm sorry."

"Can you imagine how the fuck I felt watching this shit Nephia!"

He grabbed a handful of my hair and dragged me to the French doors leading to our private terrace.

"I came home last night to be with your dumb ass. You weren't here. I called your phone, and you weren't answering. I kept calling and guess what? Your mothafuckin boyfriend answered your mothafuckin phone! Ain't that 'bout a bitch! This bitch ass nigga started talking all this shit about how he had been fucking you for years. For years! Not my mothafuckin Nephia!"

I was going to die today because he was crying as he was yelling at me. I've never seen him get this emotional in his rage.

"So this nigga sent me this goddamn video Nephia! This nigga is fucking you. He's tasting you! You liking what this nigga is doing to you. You let this nigga have you!"

"I'm sorry," I whispered.

"Get up!" he yelled as he wiped his face.

"Don't kill me," I cried.

"C'mon," he said helping me to my feet. He pushed me outside the doors.

I realized he was leading me back to his car. He did it that way because he didn't want everyone in the house to see what was going on. He made me get in. I didn't say anything. I listened to him ranting and crying. He was really fucked up about all of this. Every time the thought seemed to cross his mind, he would go into another fit of tears.

He drove us to what looked to be an old warehouse in an old industrial park.

Before we got out, he said, "I tracked where you were by your phone. And I sat outside that nigga's apartment all night. I waited for you to come out but you never did. I called Corvell and Nikki just to get a heads up on whatever lie y'all had come up with but hell they didn't even know your hoe ass hadn't come home. The whole time I was talking to you this morning I was like two cars behind you. I want you to remember that your bitch ass nigga did this. You and him. C'mon."

"Are you gonna kill me?" I cried.

"Get the fuck out the car!"

If I tried to run, I knew I wouldn't get far. I surrendered and accepted this as my fate.

I followed Marcos inside the warehouse. He led me down some stairs until we reached what looked like a boiler room. When I saw Gogo, Quan, and Mateo, I knew what this was. Once I stepped fully into the room, I saw Kendall badly beaten in a chair with his hands tied behind him.

I covered my mouth and gasped. Marcos grabbed a bat that was leaning up against the wall.

When I left Kendall's apartment, Marcos immediately started following me. He left Gogo, Quan, and Mateo to handle Kendall. While Marcos was pulling the wool over my eyes, they had Kendall and was beating the shit out of him.

Kendall lifted his head and looked at me. He said, "I'm sorry."

I was just as much to blame for this, but I couldn't fathom why he did what he did. He knew the type of person we were dealing with.

"You know why I've let you live all these years?" Marcos asked Kendall. He poked Kendall in the chest with the bat. "I never thought you would have been a threat to me. After we fucked your ass up that first time, I didn't think you would give us any more problems. But you one of them niggas that think you hard. You think you upstanding and do things the honorable way. Mothafucka you ain't shit! I wanted to kill you then, but they said, let that nigga live. But you done fucked up this time. And I'm gonna enjoy this shit."

"No!" I screamed as the bat crashed into Kendall's skull.

"No?" Marcos turned to me. "You wanna save this nigga's life?"

"Don't kill him, Marcos," I begged. I grabbed the arm that was holding the bat.

"You love him Nephia?" Marcos asked me. "Tell me you love him and I'll spare his life for you."

It was a trick question. I didn't say anything.

"You wanna take his place in that chair? I'll let him go but one of y'all or both of y'all gotta die today."

I started crying. "Please, Marcos! Don't do this!"

He pushed me away from him and swung on Kendall again. I heard bone crushing. I covered my face.

"Look at this shit! You did this!" Marcos shouted.

I couldn't look.

"Uncover your face and look at this shit!"

I stood there and watched as Marcos unleashed all of his anger on Kendall's body. I'm sure Kendall's soul left a few blows ago. I was mortified and tormented by the sight of bone and brain matter meshing together in a gruesome mangled mess of flesh. The man's eyes had come out of their sockets. This was something I would never want to witness again in this lifetime or my next one.

———————

To my surprise, Marcos didn't beat me to oblivion after that incident. He simply left. He left our home. He packed up his things and left.

Fifteen-year-old Marcena was upset. Bleu and Azul didn't really express how they felt, but I could see it in their faces that they were glad he was leaving. At thirteen it was evident that Bleu and Azul were going to be different from their father. They respected him as their father, but they despised the way Marcos treated me. Stormi and Raiyne were a little upset that their father was leaving, and six-year-old Remi just didn't understand. But Yanna was happy that he had left.

Yanna was eleven and had a sassy mouth on her. With her arms folded over her little chest and looking like her father, she said, "I don't know why you're sad Mama. When Daddy around he just make you sadder."

"Be quiet Yanna," I told her quietly.

"Do you want Daddy back?" Marcena asked.

It was just us girls. The boys had actually spent the weekend with Marcos.

I shook my head. They didn't understand my heartache. It had nothing to do with wanting Marcos. Although Kendall was foolish for doing what he did, he didn't deserve to die. And I would have forgiven him. I understood why he did what he did. And at that moment I was missing him. My despair also came from allowing myself to be in this situation.

"Is Daddy living with Brittani now?" Raiyne asked.

I had no idea where Marcos was in those days. I think he spread himself around among women. But if he had to call another place home, I'm sure he was with Terra and Brittani.

"Daddy has his own house," Marcena said. She got off my bed and kissed me on the cheek. "Well, I'm gonna get ready before Daddy gets here."

"Get ready for what? And why before your daddy get here?" I asked.

"I called him already, and when he brings Remi, Bleu, and Zuli back, I asked him if he could drop me off over Auntie Chrissy's."

"You didn't run that by me," I stated.

"I figured you wouldn't mind. Auntie Chrissy needs me to babysit," she said. She pranced out of my room with her butt-length hair flowing in the wind behind her.

Stormi and Raiyne exited next but not before giving me kisses on the cheeks. Yanna stayed and cuddled up beside me.

I laughed, "You're not sleeping in here."

"But your bed so comfortable!" Yanna whined. She inched further under my comforter.

"Okay, you can lay in here beside me and watch television but as soon as you feel yourself drifting off, get up and go to your room."

"Deal," she mumbled.

I laid quietly beside her while she went back and forward between channels. It wasn't long before Marcos, and the boys showed up. I wished he had just gotten Marcena and left. But he had to make himself be seen by me.

"Get out and go to your room," Marcos told Yanna.

She groaned and looked over at me. She looked back at him and said, "But Mama said I could stay in here until I got sleepy."

"I didn't ask for any talkback," Marcos said.

"But I wasn't talking back," Yanna said firmly.

I saw the glimmer of anger flash through Marcos's eyes. He wanted to hurt Yanna, and I wasn't going to let that happen. Before he could even get his hands on her, I covered her body with mine. "No Marcos!"

Pushing me out of the way he grabbed Yanna up by her arm while barking, "I ain't tryna hear that shit! You want your little ass beat."

"Like you do Mama!" Yanna yelled.

Marcos's grip grew tighter on her arm and literally dragged her out of bed. I jumped up and crawled out of bed as fast as I could.

"Ow!" Yanna cried out. "You're hurting me!"

"You let her go right now!" I demanded.

He did, but he basically threw her away from him causing her to stumble and fall. She looked so hurt, and I could see tears in her eyes.

189

"I'm sick of her little smart-ass mouth!" Marcos yelled. He looked at me infuriated. I couldn't figure out what I had done this time.

"She didn't do anything," I told him.

Yanna had gotten up and charged at Marcos. "I hate you! And I wish you were dead!"

I watched my child turn into the Tasmanian Devil from the Looney Tunes and unleash a series of windmill blows on Marcos.

Just as Bleu, Azul, and Stormi walked into the room, Marcos had smacked Yanna and sent her flying once again across the floor. That created a domino effect. Before I knew it, the boys were coming to their sister's defense. Yanna had snapped and was crying uncontrollably as Stormi tried consoling her.

We were all entangled in a fighting mess. I was trying to protect my kids while they were trying to beat their father's ass. The thing was, even though it was more of them, they still didn't amount to Marcos's strength.

To get his kids to calm down and gain control of the situation, he grabbed me and started choking me.

"I'ma kill her right now!" he threatened.

By this time Raiyne had come into the room and was crying with Stormi. Although I couldn't breathe, and I could feel myself slipping into unconsciousness, I could still make out the terrified looks on all of my children's faces.

Still squeezing my neck, Marcos spoke calmly to the kids, "I want y'all to get the fuck out and leave me alone with your mama. If you say one more goddamn word or come up on me like you bad, I will kill this bitch, and you'll never see her again."

"But Daddy," Stormi cried.

His grip around my neck tightened. My life was leaking from my body. I clawed at his hand desperately in need of air.

"Get the fuck out!" he yelled. Spittle flew everywhere, and the veins in his neck popped out. Even his face had turned a shade of red. "You don't fucking believe me!"

As the kids scurried out of the room, I felt his hand loosen. Before I could suck in as much air as I could, he smacked me so hard I flew into the side of the bed.

"This is why the fuck I'm gone!" he yelled at me. He came to stand over me, "Bitch I'ma kill you one day!"

I still hadn't figured out what I had done to warrant this ass whooping. I looked up into his eyes, and I realized there was no need for me to have done anything. From the look of his eyes alone and the sweat on his face, it was obvious he was high off of powder.

"I swear that little smart mouth bitch is just like your stupid ass!"

I hated when he referred to his children as anything degrading. Did he not realize they were his kids too?

I dared not say anything as I sat there pressed up against the bed. I just wanted him to leave and go wherever he was at first.

He went to the bedroom's main entrance and locked the door. I wasn't sure if I should try running for cover or what, but I was too frozen with fear.

He came back to me standing over me. He snarled, "Get

up."

Cautiously, I slid up the bed until I was able to push up off the bed and stand up. When I saw his hand swing, I put my hands up in protect mode. "I'm so sorry Marcos. Please don't hit me anymore. You know how the kids are."

"I know how they are and it's your mothafuckin' fault!" he yelled at me. "You got them thinking I'm some goddamn monster and shit. You and her started that shit with me. I had no intentions of coming in here to fuck your ass up. But since you wanna play..."

I screamed when his hand came towards me. I fell back on the bed and started sobbing heavily. "Please Marcos."

There was no sympathy for me in the way he struck me in the face.

"Please Marcos what?" he taunted menacingly. He went to strike me again.

Still crying, I stood up and grabbed him around his waist. "Please! Baby, please! I love you, and I'm tired of fighting."

He put his hands on my arm to remove me, but I clasped my hands together in a lock around his back. I placed my head against his chest and cried. "Please stop. I can't take this anymore."

I don't know what happened, but he just stood there and let me cry on him for a minute. He finally snapped out of it and snatched my arms from around him. He didn't say anything to me. He simply stormed out of the room.

Chapter 14

L illian could see the apprehension on my face. I could tell by the sad way she looked at me. From her perspective, her patient was agonizing over her home life. And I was.

"Nephia, how is this making you feel?"

"I don't know. I want him there for the kids but not for me. If it was only me, I had to think about I wouldn't want him around period."

"But do you really think having him around for the kids is what's best?" Lillian asked.

I shrugged. The kids need their father, or so that was what I had to convince myself.

"What would you like to happen with you and Marcos?"

"I don't know," I mumbled somberly.

"Do you see how he drains the energy right out of you? He's not even around as much, and he's affecting you."

"I know. I just...I just...don't know what to do."

The truth was, I was terrified. It wasn't so much as Marcos himself. I hated him and had no respect for him at this point. But I did live in fear of what he was capable of doing. It was like not being afraid of Michael Myers; however, it didn't stop him from slashing you with that big knife he carried around. And that's where I felt like things had gotten between me and Marcos.

I didn't want to go into my deepest thoughts with my therapist. Lillian would want to explore my fear. I hated when

Lillian did that. It exposed the things that I didn't want to face.

"How are things with your mother?" Lillian asked changing the subject.

"They're okay. You know my sister married that boy this past Friday," I said.

"The twenty-year-old?"

"Yep."

"Now how old is your sister again?"

"She will be twenty-nine," I answered. I shrugged carelessly, "I mean if she says she's happy then I'm happy for her. I don't wanna come off as the jealous one."

"I highly doubt that Jovelyn would accuse you of being jealous."

"She seems a lot happier than I am right now," I said with despair. Why would I be jealous of my sister's marriage? Although I felt Antoine was too young for Jovelyn, she did seem happy about her decision. I mean who was I to pass judgment on anybody's relationship?

I sighed, "But I am bitter and angry like a jealous person would be. I resent Marcos so much. But I hate myself more for being with him this long. It's 2015, and I've been with him since 1996. That's a lot of years of getting my ass whooped."

"So what are you prepared to do?" she asked. I had no answer to give. She leaned forward in her seat and said, "You know, you're the only one that can put an end to all of this."

Tears came to my eyes. "I don't want to hurt the kids."

"They'll be understanding. The boys don't really like him much anyway. Your twin daughters don't know how to feel about him. Your one daughter can't stand him. The oldest daughter is the only one who has any sympathy for him."

"I wish he would just get help and be what he needs to be for me and the kids."

"Obviously that isn't something he wants. He would have cleaned up his act years ago."

I already knew that. There was no hope for Marcos. It seemed he had gotten worse. He was in the house with us again, but he wasn't really in the house. I barely saw him twice out of a week. He ripped and ran in the streets. He would leave the states to spend a lot of time with his father too. God knows what he was doing during those times. When he did come around, it was to make me miserable. He had gotten better with the kids and stopped being physical with me in front of them. But it was the little things that he tormented me with. It was like instead of breaking me down with physical abuse, he attacked me with words. He threatened to take my lifestyle away. He held taking custody of the kids over my head. He would remind me that without him I would be nothing. And he would let me know that he shouldn't have married me and he felt stuck with me. And since he was stuck with me, I was the one that would suffer for it.

My spirits had dropped so low, I knew I *had* to seek therapy. I was on antidepressants, and they didn't seem like they worked. Most days I plastered a smile on my face and pretended I was okay, but inside I wanted to die.

Lillian looked at me with empathy. "This is not good for you Nephia. And I'm concerned for you. I really am."

I was pitiful. I despised myself for being so weak. Maybe I deserved to be treated this way. I began to cry. I cried, and I cried until my body shook. Lillian didn't know what to say to console me. I became hysterical. I literally had a breakdown in her office.

Because of her concern, she called mobile crisis. She didn't trust me with my self. Once I got to the hospital, I let them do whatever they wanted to do. I didn't put up much of a fight. And the more I thought of my kids and how weak I was, the more I wept.

———————

Two weeks later I was discharged from the psychiatric hospital. I was a lot better coming out than I was going in, but I had a long journey of recovery ahead of me.

I was happy to see my best friends Corvell and Nikki when I walked off the elevator and into the lobby of the psychiatric hospital.

"Bring yo' crazy ass on here!" Corvell laughed.

I chuckled placing my finger up to my lips to hush him. "Ssh. You can't be saying that around here like that."

"It's a fucking mental hospital. They know they crazy," Corvell argued. He reached for my overnight bag I had on my shoulder.

"You look good," Nikki beamed.

"Thanks," I said. I followed them out of the building to the parking lot.

Once inside Corvell's car, I said, "Well, I guess it's back to life."

Nikki looked back at me. "I guess this was like a little vacation away from home."

"A vacation?" I laughed. "Hardly. Some of those people in there are crazy as hell. And all it did was make me feel even more fucked up. Like, I'm in here with these crazy mothafuckas! And then this one boy and girl got caught fucking up in there."

"What?" Nikki snickered.

"Then my roommate kept shoving pictures of her kids and grandkids in my face every chance she got and talking about how people thought she was faking being bipolar. There was a Russian chick in there that was on chill the whole time. She had crying spells out of the blue though. Then there was an older black lady that reminded me of Ada. She stabbed her husband with a pencil!"

On the drive to my house, I told them all kind of stories of my two-week stay. I even told them about some of the things I had discovered about myself. I never realized I had been suffering from depression ever since I was a child. I've always felt the blues. Marcos was my trigger and a catalyst. I had to get rid of him if I wanted to live a more fulfilling life.

Of course, my closest family and friends wouldn't be them if they didn't have a small welcome home get together waiting for my arrival. My kids bombarded me with hugs and kisses.

"We miss you so much!" Stormi and Raiyne both said in their dramatic manner.

"I miss y'all too," I smiled.

"How you feeling?" Ada asked with her warm smile. To be in her sixties, this woman still looked the same way she did when I first met her almost twenty years ago.

"I'm better," I told her.

"Mama, we made the cake for you," Remi beamed.

"Well, not all by ourselves," Yanna corrected. "*Lola*, Granny, and Ms. Ada helped us."

I looked over at Lailani and Beverly and smiled. These two women were me at one point. They survived. The question posed: Would I?

I was enjoying my home welcoming until Marcos showed up with Quan and Gogo. They helped themselves to the food that was prepared for this get-together. It amazed me how Marcos could show up to crash my little party but was nowhere to be found when I was discharged from the hospital.

I was sitting at the kitchen counter on one of the barstools looking at them with disgust.

"Why the fuck you looking like that?" Marcos asked with a snarl. "You looking like we stank or something."

I didn't say anything.

"Is you drunk?" Ada asked Marcos jokingly. "You high or something. Get on out of my kitchen with all that."

I know she was trying to calm him before anything exploded. That was why I remained quiet. I did ask Gogo, "Where's Bridgette and how is she?"

Before Gogo could answer, Marcos walked upon me and mushed my head. "Who the fuck told you to get your ass confined to a mothafuckin' crazy house? Are you stupid? Or is that your way of fucking with me?"

I swatted at his hand that kept jabbing at my head for emphasis. "Leave me alone Marcos. This ain't the time, okay?"

"When is the time?"

I agreed with Ada. Marcos showed up here high. I could see it in his eyes, and the beads of sweat around his hairline were telltale signs.

"You're a dumb ass bitch, you know that?"

"And you're high," I mumbled.

Beverly tried to step in to diffuse the situation. "Marcos, baby let me show you what I was talking about in my—"

Marcos ignored his mother completely. He went to jab at my head again, and as a reflex, I smacked the shit out of his hand. He retaliated by smacking me with his open hand. Shocked and angered, I swung on him. At this point, Gogo, Lailani, and Beverly intervened to keep him from fully attacking me. I managed to hop off the stool and headed to my bedroom. I could hear Marcos shouting out obscenities to hurt my feelings, but I was too focused on not crying.

Stormi came into the room behind me. "You okay Mama?"

"I'm fine," I said with a sigh. I laid across the bed.

Stormi lay beside me. "Sorry, Daddy ruin your welcome home party."

"But it was nice still," I told her.

Stormi began lovingly finger-combing my hair. "Mama, I think Daddy is sick."

I looked at her blankly. I mentioned before that I named Stormi and Raiyne their names because of the weather outside at the time I pushed them into the world. However, Stormi had this sixth sense that was really weird. When she said things like what she just said, it usually came to be. It's like her name took on a second meaning as if to say a storm is brewing, weather the storm, or the calm before the storm. A prediction so to speak.

"Why do you say that?"

She gave a half shrug. "He acts sick. Sometimes he looks sick."

That was the effects of his drug use and drinking. I chuckled to myself. "Then I agree with you. He is sick."

"No," she shook her head. "He smells sick."

Maybe if I had actually taken heed of what she was trying to tell me this day. I don't know. It probably wouldn't have changed what was to come, but I could have been more prepared...if I had known.

Chapter 15

I don't know why I listened to Nikki and her cousin Penny. At first, I thought it was ridiculous to use a dating app on my phone to meet people. But Nikki was always telling me about Penny's newfound beau she discovered on the app. Nikki herself had met a couple of guys she communicated with but none of those turned out to be much of a success, yet she told me to give it a try.

After making a public profile, my notifications piled up almost immediately. I got several inbox messages. I went through each of them. The ones that couldn't construct a simple sentence or greet me appropriately were ignored. I spoke back to a few of them, but they were boring. Once I checked out their profiles, there was nothing that really piqued my interests. But for the time being, I would just enjoy this as entertainment; something to occupy my time and distract my mind from my home life. I wasn't crazy enough to actually try to meet another guy. Not after what Marcos did to Kendall.

"What the fuck you looking at?"

The sound of his voice irritated me. Lately, it annoyed me for him to even talk to me. After my stay in the hospital, he came home and made sure that I rarely smiled. Marcos was getting worse, and I was beginning to allow myself not to love him. I mean, he didn't want me. He didn't love me. Why couldn't he just let me go?

Careful not to alert him to my activities, I offered him a small smile, "Nikki is texting me. She wants me to go—"

"You ain't going nowhere," he interrupted.

"I wasn't planning to," I assured him.

201

He cut his eyes towards me as he made his way to his closet.

"Are you going somewhere?" I asked. When he didn't respond, I posed another question. "Have you booked those rappers for the boys' party yet?"

He stepped back out of the closet wearing a fresh and crisp white button-down shirt. "You just worry about what you're supposed to do for their party."

I mumbled, "I was just asking because you forget sometimes."

His eyes shifted to my phone. I casually let it slip towards me as I hit the home button. And as I suspected, in a swift motion, Marcos had snatched my phone from me.

Nicely, I asked, "Can I have my phone back?"

Ignoring me, he began tapping on it. I'm sure he went to my messages and read that Nikki certainly asked me to go out with her and the gang. I smiled because I'm always a step ahead of him now. The dating app wasn't even visible on any of my screens.

Marcos tossed my phone back to me and cut his eyes at me. "Tell that bitch you ain't coming."

As soon as he turned his back, I rolled my eyes. To ensure he was leaving, I jumped out of bed and followed slowly behind him out of the bedroom. I went to the kitchen where Yanna, Stormi, and Raiyne were actively destroying it.

"What are y'all doing?" I asked as I took inventory of the mess they were making.

Yanna grinned holding up a mixing spoon with thick batter adorning it. "We making homemade cookies!"

"Y'all make sure you get this shit up too," Marcos barked over his shoulder as he exited the kitchen through the door leading to the garage.

Like me, Yanna knew to roll her eyes behind his back. She still couldn't stand her father. The other kids tolerated him and still adored him on his good days. Yanna didn't care if it was a good day or a great day; she didn't trust him or respect him. And I never tried to convince her otherwise. She was old enough to know and understand how she felt about him. So be it.

"Hey, Mama."

I looked up to see Bleu entering the kitchen. The expression on his face wasn't sitting well with me. He looked bothered; somewhat worried.

"Can I talk to you?" he asked. I noticed he didn't bother to give me any eye contact.

Usually, I would tease him, but this seemed serious. "Sure," I told him.

We walked out of the kitchen and into the formal dining room.

Bleu didn't waste any time getting to it. He blurted out, "Shana's pregnant."

"Huh?"

He finally looked at me and repeated. "Shana's pregnant."

"What Shana?" I asked. I was dumbfounded and refused to believe he was talking about his little white friend that happened to be a female.

"*Shana*, Shana," he said with emphasis.

"Pregnant?" I still wasn't trying to catch on.

He nodded.

I stared at him as my heart began to drop. The look he gave me told it all. I let out a devastated groan and took a seat at the dining room table. So many things swarmed through my head. I thought about how I didn't want my kids, none of them to experience any of the horrid things I had to endure when I was younger. I thought of me not being a good parent. I didn't want him to be another me. I was a teenage parent. I didn't want this for him!

"Bleu," I groaned.

He sat down a seat away from me. "I'm sorry Mama."

"Sorry is right!" I exclaimed.

"But Mama—"

"No!" I interrupted him. I wanted to be mad and smack some sense into him but what point would that make? Taking a few deep breaths, calmly I asked, "Do her parents know?"

He nodded.

"How far along is she?"

He shrugged.

"You don't know!" I snapped.

"She doesn't know. She never got her period."

"When was her period supposed to come?"

"December or January I think," he told me.

Flabbergasted, I yelled, "December or Jan—Bleu! This is June!"

"I know," he mumbled.

Now I was mad. "Why hadn't her mama called me yet?"

"Because her mama doesn't know who she's pregnant by."

"Hell, does she know who's she pregnant by?" I asked.

"Me."

I gave him a scolding look. "So you're proudly claiming it, huh?"

"Shana is not like that Mama," he countered.

I don't know who Shana was when she wasn't around me. What I've gathered from the times she has been around us, Shana was a well behaved quiet girl. But she still had a sneakiness about her that I have grown to associate with white girls because of Marcos. Bleu just had to be like his father and have a thing for white girls or very light skinned black girls. His brother Azul, on the other hand, liked them chocolate.

"Have you told your daddy?" I asked.

He shook his head.

I chuckled while shaking my head. "Marcos might give you a pat on the back."

"Or beat me," Bleu added quietly.

I shot him a look. "He won't do that. He of all people know he doesn't have a right to be mad at you."

"There's a lot of things Daddy don't have a right to do, but he does them anyway."

Was that a dig? Whatever it was, it made me feel uncomfortable. It was my guilt. My kids shouldn't be exposed to Marcos' behavior. He's warping their way of thinking. He's destroying their innocence. Will my girls be afraid to ever date a man or will they think it's okay to be in a relationship like the one their parents were in? Will Bleu feel like he can do whatever he wants without much consideration of someone else's feelings?

I sighed heavily, "I'm disappointed, but we'll get through this. I'll talk with Shana's mother, and we'll go from there."

Bleu nodded. He got up from the table wearing a more relieved expression. He even smiled when he gave me a hug and pecked my cheek before he left out of the dining room.

I tapped my phone on the table as I fell deep in thought. Damn, was I about to be a grandmother? I was barely thirty-three! More shit on top of more shit.

I went to my dating app on my phone and saw that I had eighteen new messages. I quickly went through the first twelve and responded. I got to the thirteenth one and paused. Now, what the hell was this man doing on here! He was too fine to be on some dating app. I know he had to get the panties thrown at him at least six times a day.

Blake0524 had a thuggish quality about him that had my cat whining. His soft brown complexion contrasted nicely with his mustache and a full beard that was so neatly trimmed and edged, it almost looked fabricated. He had deep-set brown eyes, thick eyebrows, and long lashes. His lips were nicely shaped, not too full but definitely not thin. I loved his hair too. It wasn't exactly cut low because I could see the curl pattern even in his photo. He had a little offside part that screamed pretty boy, but that burly beard screamed pretty boy with a little thug in him.

The funny thing was, his message read: **You're a beautiful woman and according to your profile, you seem to have a lot to bring to any table. I'm curious as**

to why you're even a member?

I laughed aloud. I responded: **I could ask you the same thing**

Waiting for him to reply I hopped over to my text messages to send Nikki and Corvell a group text: **Bleu got that white girl pregnant.**

Corvell: I **knew she was around for some black dick!**

Nikki: **Really Corvell?**

Corvell: **Did Zuli hit it too?**

Me: **Zuli don't like white meat**

Nikki: **What did Marcos say?**

Me: **He doesn't know yet**

I switched back to the dating app. Blake0524: **It's something to do...passing time**

I smiled as I typed back: **But being on here isn't really necessary for you to pass time...I know you have several women throwing themselves at you that will give you something to do**

It showed that he read my message, but I hopped back over to Corvell and Nikki.

Nikki: **What is wrong with Bleu? Tbh I would have thought it was Zuli's lil fast tail**

Corvell: **That's what I'm saying!**

Corvell: **But Bleu is a softy**

Nikki: **What that mean?**

Corvell: **He be all in love and shit**

Me: **Are we forgetting we're talking about my fifteen year old son?**

Corvell: **What fifteen got to do with anything...That boy been fucking!**

I shook my head. I went back to the app.

Blake0524: **I do have a few options. Someone suggested it to me, and I made a profile. I check it from time to time. If a profile interests me, I'll consider reaching out. I saw yours and here I am**

Me: **Yeah I guess the same applies to me**

While I waited for him to reply I gave his profile a quick scan. His profile headline was, "One day at a time." He was thirty-five, six feet even, a Christian, had kids, not a smoker but drink, a Gemini, looking for friendship, the longest relationship was a year, and one of his interests was dancing. That only caught my eye because it's what I do. His occupation was: Business owner. His first date was: *Let's talk and see what we can come up with.*

Not only was he attractive but his profile seemed rather nice. I was curious about why his longest relationship had only been a year, but he had kids. I kept looking at his pictures. I was beginning to think he was a total catfish although his profile came off as genuine. He probably grabbed these pics from somebody's Facebook page.

I typed: **Your profile is nice**

I went to my text messages.

Nikki: **Are you getting the baby tested to make sure?**

Me: **Of course but Bleu seems sure it's his**

Corvell: **He gon haveta get a J.O.B. now…Or are you gonna continue to spoil him?**

Me: **No, he will have to be responsible now. There's another p—**

Before I could even finish typing, my phone was snatched from behind me. I whipped around fast to see Marcos glaring at the screen of my phone. Where did he come from? How did I not hear him?

"What the fuck y'all talking about?" he asked. He didn't give me time to reply. His eyes were glowering. "What is this Neph?"

"It's Bleu," I answered as I stood.

"Who asked you to get up? Sitcho ass back down," he ordered.

I did as I was told.

"So Bleu got that girl pregnant?" he asked. His tone was as if I were the one that was in trouble.

"Yeah," I mumbled.

"So when the fuck was you gonna tell me!" he barked as he stepped closer to me.

I flinched thinking he was about to hit me. "I just found out. He just told me."

With my phone still in his hand, he turned to head out. I jumped up to follow him. He pivoted to face me with an intimidating stare. "Did I tell you to get up?"

"No, but Marcos, don't go in—"

He smacked me so hard I know I did a three-sixty spin.

"You stay your ass in here," he hissed before walking out of the dining room yelling for Bleu.

I hoped he wouldn't go to Bleu to do as he feared. Stormi and Yanna walked into the dining room looking concerned.

"What happened Mama?" Stormi asked.

"What did Bleu do?" Yanna wanted to know.

I shook my head. "Don't worry about it. Y'all just go—"

"Did he hit you?" Yanna asked incredulously.

"Yanna," I said firmly. "Just go back to the kitchen and finish baking cookies with your sister."

The girls reluctantly headed out of the dining room. I stood there listening for any signs of a scuffle. There was no scuffle, but I could hear Marcos yelling.

I hope my phone was no longer of importance. And when I got it back, I had to make sure I deleted that dating app.

———————

The following day, I spoke with Shana's mother, Claire. She nor Shana had an issue with us wanting a blood test. Marcos insisted on it. Bleu thought it was insulting to Shana, but he didn't voice that to Marcos. He barely wanted to speak to Marcos after being smacked around for being "so stupid."

Drowning out my problems, I focused on the kids in the school's summer program. When I was here, Marcos didn't exist unless he showed up to pretend to be such a good husband and father. Other than that I lost myself in dance, the kids' laughter, and socializing with the rest of the staff.

"Mrs. B!"

The recognition of her voice put a smile on my face. I

purposely took my time turning around to address her.

"Mrs. B! You hear me. Is you ignoring me? You know that's rude right Mrs. B?"

I giggled and finally faced my little friend. "And how are you Special K?"

The six-year-old grinned proudly. I was pleasantly surprised and shocked to see she had lost both her top front teeth. I gasped excitedly, "Where are your teeth?"

She giggled, even more, making her cherubic cheeks rise causing her already slanted eyes to thin out.

"They came out," she explained.

"Did you get a visit from the tooth fairy?" I asked.

Her smile faded, and she gave me a "yeah right" type of look. Flatly she said, "My daddy said the tooth fairy lost her key to our house, so she didn't get in last night."

I laughed. "What?"

She placed her hand on her little hip. "He knows I don't believe him. Toothfairies don't even use keys. Who he think I'm is Mrs. B?"

I loved this little girl. She was one of the most outgoing students in the entire school. She loved talking and would carry on a conversation like she was an adult. She made my day.

"I don't know, but he better recognize!" I said egging her on.

"Hey, little lady!" Omar called out from the studio's entrance. "Let's go. We're about to start."

She smiled up at me, her dark eyes twinkling. "Well, I

guess I'll see you later. I got some new dance moves too. I'ma show you before I leave."

"Okay. Can't wait," I told her. I watched her skip out of the studio. Her thick ponytails swung behind her. She was the prettiest little chocolate girl I had ever laid eyes on. It didn't help that she had such a cute, spunky personality.

I retrieved my phone from the window sill. I never got around to deleting the app the day before. I knew I needed to, but before I removed it, I took a peek at my messages. Why did I blush when I saw there were two unread messages from Blake0524. I went through all of them and saved his for last on purpose.

Blake0524: **Yours is too which is baffling**

Blake0524: **Okay, maybe you are looking for a man on here, maybe not but I'm curious to know why this route. Are you one of those cursed women like Halle Barry who's so beautiful she have no luck when it come to men? I mean, there's some nice looking women on here but that's all they seem to be able to offer. You're different.**

I decided to respond since it showed he was currently online: **Hey sorry I didn't respond to you last night. I got caught up. And I don't think I'm cursed...I can be the first to admit that I need to open myself up to what else is out there**

To my surprise, he responded right away.

Blake0524: **I was beginning to think you were ignoring me. What do you mean open yourself up?**

Me: **I'm closed off. I'm afraid. I don't even know why I made this profile because I'm not going to do**

212

anything with it

Blake0524: **Why not? You're here now. Might as well make use of it**

Me: **Most of the guys on here are like predators and too aggressive for me**

Blake0524: **You've been hurt**

Me: **Yeah I have**

Blake0524: **So have I**

Me: **Recently?**

Blake0524: **It's been over a year now but it's still there**

I didn't know this guy, but my heart was going out to him. It drew me in more, and I felt compelled to keep talking to him.

Blake0524: **How long has it been for you?**

I couldn't really answer that question honestly. My heartbreak was a present ever-going situation.

Me: **It's been very recent. It was why my friend suggested I go on this app just to see what else is out there.**

Blake0524: **Yeah, I'm skeptical of these things but I've heard some have been really successful at finding love this way**

Me: **Yeah my friend's cousin seem to have found the love of her life**

Blake0524: **How many of those do a person get?**

Me: **What?**

Blake0524: **Love of their life**

That was a question I've never pondered on. Was Marcos the love of my life? Of course not. Was the love of my life still out there? Perhaps Kendall had been it. I let my mind drift into memories of him. I wished he was still around. He used to be what I needed after a few weeks of Marcos' abuse. I cherished the days Kendall would pamper me and make love to me. Why did he do what he did? So many days I wished I could go back to that night and do things differently just to spare his life.

Me: **I don't know. I'm not sure if I've ever crossed paths with mine**

Blake0524: **So have you not ever been in love?**

I shook my head as if he could see me. The answer was like a revelation to me. What does "in love" feel like? I mean, is it the same kind of love I have for my kids? I'm totally in love with them. They are my everything even though I feel as though I fail them as a mother.

Me: **I don't think I have...not with a man at least**

Blake0524: **With a woman?**

I laughed: **Lol...no. I mean i'm in love with my kids**

Blake0524: **lol...gotcha. That kind of love. How many do you have?**

Me: 7

Blake0524: **Stop messing with me lady. Either you're playing or those are not your pictures on this profile**

Me: **Why do you say that? That's me and I have 7 kids. And I know 7 kids is a lot for any man to**

consider playing stepdad to which is another reason I'm guarded. I'm sure your interest has plummeted

Blake0524: **I'm amazed actually. You're beautiful anyway but to know you have 7 kids....Just wow!**

Me: **So you're still interested?**

Blake0524: **The fact that you have kids isn't a turn off. Hell, I'm a single dad to three.**

Me: **Really?**

Blake0524: **Yes really. I have a request**

Me: **What?**

Blake0524: **Can we speak over the phone?**

I know my actions were asking for an ass whooping but I was really drawn to this person. I loved the interaction. I gave him my number, and within seconds an unfamiliar number was calling my phone. I was hesitant to answer it at first. It was my nerves. "Hello?"

"So you gave me the right number."

His voice did something to me. A smile so big spread across my face and just stayed there. Pretending not to know who was calling me, I asked, "Who is this?"

"You know who this is and whatchu' smiling for? I hear it all in your lil sexy voice."

I caught my bottom lip in between my teeth as if I was some little school girl. I was trying to control the smile that had taken over my face. I finally asked, "What's your name?"

"What it say on my profile?"

"Nothing. Your real name isn't on there. You just have

your profile name on there."

"Then that's my name."

"So you want me to call you Blake zero five two four?"

"You can just call me Blake. Is Filipinobeauty your real name?" he asked with a hint of humor in his voice.

I thought it over. If he were someone that knew Marcos, then he would have recognized me from the pictures. I decided to tell him my real name. "You can call me Nephia."

"Nephia," he echoed as if he was familiarizing himself with the way my name formed in his mouth. "That's different. Is it Filipino?"

"It is."

"What percentage of Filipino are you?"

"Just fifty."

"Your mother?"

"Yeah, it's her," I chuckled lightly.

"Back to what we were talking about but first—I'm not holding you up from anything, am I?"

I said, "No, you're fine. I got a few minutes to spare." For the first time, I paid attention to his background. It was rather noisy as if he was outside.

"What are your kids' ages?" he asked.

"They range in age from eighteen to eight. Four girls and three boys. Two sets of twins; a pair of boys and a pair of girls. What about you?"

"Twins? How interesting. I have an eight-year-old son, a six-year-old daughter, and a two-month-old son."

If he and I were seriously pursuing something with one another, him having a two-month-old son would bother me. It would definitely be a red flag.

"You have a two-month-old son?"

"Yep."

"And you're not with the mother?"

"No. It ain't like that. Shit just happened, and he's here. But we ain't in no relationship or nothing like that."

"Two months...that's really fresh."

"That bothers you?"

"With a baby that little I'm sure the mother is still close by."

"She is close by but...we're co-parenting."

His answer didn't come off as confident as the rest of his responses. I think it was safe for me to assume that he and his baby mama were still "involved."

I asked, "Why didn't you two work out? Y'all had three kids together and—"

His laughter interrupted me. "No. She's not the mother of all three."

"Oh."

"Yeah, I got baby mamas."

I wasn't trying to judge him at all. As a matter of fact, I commended him for taking his role in his children's life so seriously.

Changing the subject, I said, "You know you're a really nice looking guy according to your profile. How do I know you're not catfishing me?"

"And you're not catfishing me?"

"Do you have an iPhone?" I asked.

"Yeah, I do."

We hung up, and I called him back via Facetime. When he answered something weird happened. Neither one of us said anything. We just smiled goofily. I could sense that he was just as relieved as I was that we were who we claimed to be on our profiles. He was even more fine to me. His facial hair wasn't as neat as the pictures, but there was a ruggedness that turned me on.

I noticed that he was in a vehicle. I asked, "Are you on your way somewhere?"

"No," he answered. He gave me a light smile and said, "I'm sorry, but you're a lot more beautiful than your pictures made you out to be."

"Thank you," I blushed.

"If you're interested still, I'd like to continue to get to know you more."

I nodded with a smile. "Yeah."

"Not rushing or anything."

"No, no...no rushing."

"Good," he said.

It was then I noticed that he had a sweet smile, but it ended just at his lips. His eyes held so much sadness. There was no twinkle there at all. I wondered if the same sadness I saw in his face was the same that people saw in me. It was heart-wrenching. I suddenly empathized with him, and my heart went out to him. I wanted to know Blake. I wanted to know what caused him to hurt.

Something or someone caught his attention causing him to turn to look out the window. His masculinity captivated me. I could look at him all day. And he had these extremely long lashes that should have been against the law. I mean, women were out here paying good money to have lashes like his.

When he turned back to the screen, I felt both embarrassed and ashamed for taking such enjoyment in staring at him.

"Hey, I gotta go but don't be a stranger. Okay?" he said to me.

"I won't," I said.

"Okay. Take care beautiful."

"Bye," I quietly said before ending the connection.

What have I started? I can't do this again. However, that void inside was so hollow that loneliness echoed off its walls. I wanted to experience love from a true man. And maybe Blake wasn't him, but this encounter was awakening something within.

Chapter 16

I was lying to Blake. I think he knew I was lying. He never asked me, but I think he assumed I had a man even though I assured him I was single.

Our communication had been going on for two weeks. Even if it was a simple text to say "hey," we didn't go a day without some kind of contact. A few days we had talked during lunch for about thirty minutes over the phone. The rest of the time we would text back and forward. I was always nervous that he would call when Marcos was around but so far he hadn't. He never called me without waiting for me to respond to his text that he sent out first. I told him the kids usually kept me busy in the evenings, so I think he was trying to respect my time.

Marcos was nowhere to be found. Things between us were becoming non-existent. I was grateful for it. I loved that he didn't feel a need to have sex with me anymore. I was glad someone else was taking care of that. I no longer desired to be with Marcos in that way. Every day some kind of thought entered my mind that he would die in a freak accident. I was trying to will it to happen, but with my luck, I'm sure Marcos would be around to make sure I was unhappy.

In the meantime, I looked forward to hearing from Blake. This particular Saturday night, I actually felt safe enough to talk to him over the phone.

Curled up comfortably in bed, I asked, "So you're not going out?"

"I don't go out every weekend. This is my weekend with my kids. They gotta get some uninterrupted time with Daddy too."

"I bet your daughter is so spoiled."

"She's no Daddy's princess."

"She isn't?"

He laughed. "No. She acts like she's my mama. She's a trip though."

"I can't imagine you with a bossy little girl."

"Why is that?"

"You're so passive and soft-spoken."

"That's funny because those words have never been used to describe me before."

"But that's how you come off to me. You're usually not passive?"

"I guess I can be but...I don't know. I guess life has knocked me back a little."

"Life has humbled you? Is that what you're saying?"

"No, not humble. Life has taken a big chunk of me," he answered. His voice filled with melancholy and sorrow. "Spiritually and emotionally I guess. Some days I don't know if I'll ever experience happiness the same way I once had before."

I think I understood exactly what he was saying. "I don't think I've ever experienced happiness the way I probably should have. I've been through so much."

"Are we even healthy for one another?" he asked with a chuckle.

"Probably not. Two broken people can't fix each other."

"Why are you so broken? What did he do?"

I was a little thrown off by his question. Talking about Marcos was something I was avoiding. I wasn't ready to bring any of that up with Blake. I guess he could sense my trouble and hesitation.

"You don't have to talk about it if you're not comfortable."

"Not yet," I mumbled.

"A little at a time."

I smiled. Maybe we were two broken people who were unhealthy for one another if we were trying to pursue a relationship. But what I appreciated about Blake was that he was there, and he was someone other than my therapist that listened and sympathized.

"Thanks for talking to me Blake. I wanna be able to see you in person one day."

"I don't know if that's a good idea," he said. I could hear the playfulness returning to his voice.

"Why is that?"

"My attraction to you is definitely serious but at the same time, I would wanna respect you as the friend that you're becoming. But talking to you and seeing you when we Facetime is like torture."

"Torture?"

"Yeah, I might be emotionally broken, but other parts of me still work well."

I couldn't resist snickering at his comment. I knew exactly what he meant. Hell, my lady parts came alive whenever I heard his voice or saw his name on my phone.

"You're so silly," I told him.

"But we might be able to make that happen one day. Just be sure that you will be comfortable. Don't rush none of this."

"Definitely don't wanna rush."

"I think I hear lil man waking up. If I can, I'll text you later."

I was almost disappointed that he had to get off the phone. "Okay."

———————

A few days later I found myself daydreaming about my first encounter with Blake. I know I would be nervous and it might be awkward. I wondered if he would even try to be sexual with me. He didn't come off as the type which was another thing that had me drawn to him. Blake seemed to be a gentleman, but that was only what he showed me over the phone. For all, I know he could be another Marcos in disguise.

Snapping out of my daydream, I became aware that Marcos was staring at me. There was a look of anger in disgust in his eyes. I blinked back at him wondering what I had done now.

It was the morning, and I didn't have much time to entertain his craziness. I had to get ready for work and wake the kids. His crazy ass had just come home after the break of dawn, and he wanted to start some shit.

Ignoring him, I headed to the bathroom to get myself together. He followed me and continued to stare at me while I brush my teeth. I avoided looking in the mirror at his reflection.

Leaning up against the inside of the doorframe, he

frowned. "What have you been up to lately?"

I wanted to tell him he would know if he would be a husband and father and stay home sometimes. But I realized a while ago that commenting with smart comebacks wouldn't get me very far.

I didn't answer him until after I gave my teeth a quick scan for approval. I looked at him through the mirror as I began to wash my face. "Nothing. Just working and being a mom."

"Yeah," he scoffed while nodding his head knowingly.

I didn't let him bother me. After I was done, I tried to head out, but he acted as if he didn't want to get out of my way. I gave him a look. "Can I get by please?"

He moved just enough so that I could squeeze by. I went into my closet to dress for the day. I didn't have to turn around to know that he had followed me. I could feel him in the closet with me.

"So you done started locking your phone again," he stated as an observation.

I continued to layer myself in clothing trying to remain as private with it as possible. I'm not quite sure what it was, but I didn't like being fully naked before him anymore. It was almost as if he didn't have a right to see me in such a way. I no longer felt like I belonged to him.

"You not gonna say nothing?"

I looked up at him. "Oh...I didn't realize you were asking me. But yeah, I've started locking my phone again. The kids be grabbing my phone and accidentally read the stuff Corvell be saying in his texts. You know he don't censor himself."

"Are you sure it's the shit Corvell say you don't want them

to see?" He gave me a menacing glare. "Or maybe you don't want them to see they're mama talking to another nigga."

What was he talking about now? My aggravation must have shown on my face.

He said, "So you wanna play dumb?"

"What are you talking about?" I asked. I tried to remain calm while slipping on my capris. Had to remain alert and aware of any sudden movements.

"What's the code?"

I called it off to him without hesitation. While he searched for whatever it was he thought he had on me, I took my time deciding what pair of shoes I wanted to wear.

"Somebody said they saw you on some dating shit."

I didn't break my stride because I have no idea what he's talking about.

"You meeting niggas and shit now Neph?"

I stood to my full height completely clothed. I said with confidence, "No, I'm not. Who told you that anyway?"

"Don't worry about it. They said they saw you on it though."

"Really?" I asked. My mind running rapid trying to recall if anyone I came across on the dating app looked familiar. I challenged, "Did you see me on it?"

"Naw, but—"

"Okay then," I said smartly. I proceeded to walk by him, but he didn't allow me to pass.

"Where the shit at?" he asked. He handed my phone over,

"Show me."

"Show you what?" I asked.

"Pull the shit up."

"There's nothing to pull up. I'm not on anything. Now if whoever said they saw me on there why didn't they have proof to show you? Why would you even come to me with mess like that and not—"

I was interrupted by him grasping my face around my mouth and giving a reinforcing squeeze.

"Don't question me!" he snapped. "I can come at you any fucking way I feel. You're my wife! You belong to me. What the fuck you mean? And let me find out you lying being sneaky covering your tracks and shit! I'ma fuck you up Neph!"

I tried to force his hand away by pulling on his arm. Then I began trying to connect my phone with his knuckles hoping to cause him enough pain to let me go. The more I resisted, the harder he squeezed. I couldn't do anything but look him in the eyes and hope that he would let me go.

Marcos held my gaze as a sinister grin formed on his lips. He let me go with a push to my head. "You look so fucking pathetic."

I didn't just look it; I was pathetic. How much more of this was I going to go through? I asked myself that question over and over. When would the day come that I've had enough and leave? Or when would the day come that he get it over with and just kill me?

"Are you done?" Where did those words come from? Did I just ask him that? Why?

He was about to walk away, but he paused, looked back at

me, and said, "You must want me to beat your ass."

"Hey, you don't love me if you ain't beating me," I said sarcastically. I offered him a forced smile.

He actually chuckled at my foolishness. It wasn't one of those chuckles that he thought what I said was funny, but rather one that let me know he was getting annoyed. Maybe I should stop while I was ahead.

Marcos cut his eyes at me before walking away. Inside I sighed with relief.

Walking back out into the bedroom, I went for my purse sitting on the chaise lounge. Marcos was sitting at the foot of our bed and was on the phone. I paused when I heard him say, "Hey Mama, can you let them know Neph won't be in for the day. Get somebody else to cover for her."

Frowned up in confusion, I looked at him. "Why are you telling her I'm not coming to work?"

Instead of asking questions, I should have been running for the door. In two seconds, Marcos was able to end the phone call while getting up and striking me with more force than necessary. It sent me bouncing against our bed. Holding my face from the sting of the blow and shock, I looked up at him with question.

He began to explain in a very cold tone, "Since you wanna be smart and shit, I thought I'd give you what you want. And—"

"No! You're upset because you didn't find out what—"

"Shut the fuck up!" he barked and went to hit me again.

I blocked him from hitting my face, but he tried getting punches in between my arms.

"Get up!" he ordered.

I used the edge of the nightstand to assist me to my feet. And at that moment I got the bright idea to do like they do in the movies and grab the lamp to swing on him. In mid-swing I knew I had fucked up, but I also knew I couldn't undo my move.

It didn't do what I wanted it to do, but it did connect upside his head enough to shock him. I didn't wait this time. I sprinted for the bedroom door before he could grab me.

I had no idea where I was running to. I couldn't leave because I never picked my purse up from the chaise lounge. I had no keys, but I was still holding on to my phone. Never looking back to see if he was following me, I hurried down the stairs to our lower level. I could hear him coming, but he wasn't that close. I quickly dashed behind the bar in the recreational room. There was a cabinet back there that the kids would hide inside when they were playing around. Thankful that I was still petite, I eased inside and carefully closed the doors.

I heard him. He was downstairs with me. He didn't seem pressed to find me. He was taking his time, taunting me with his casual stroll and whistling.

"You always wanna play games Neph. So we'll play. But when I find you or whenever you decide to come out of hiding, I'ma beat your ass."

Why won't he just go away! I didn't get why he still felt a need to be around just to make me miserable. Why?

"Marcos!"

He ignored Ada calling for him. He came around the bar, and I knew he knew where I was. I was just waiting for him to open the door.

"Marcos! It's your mama calling. She said it's important!"

I held my breath just so he couldn't hear me.

Ada yelled in the distance, "It's your grandmama! She done died! Your daddy just called."

"What?" Marcos exclaimed. I could hear the panic in his voice.

I know this was an evil thought, but I had never been so happy to hear about somebody's death as I was at that moment. Just like that, Marcos abandoned his pursuit of killing me.

Saved by death.

———

Marcos went to Columbia along with Beverly, Chrissy, and four out of our seven kids. Bleu and Azul stayed behind because they had prior plans to travel to Miami with a friend and his family for the Fourth of July holiday. And Yanna just didn't want to go. She didn't like her father or any of his family.

Of course, we got into an argument which reminded him he owed me an ass whooping already. As a reminder of who he was and as assurance that I had no plans to go out for the holiday while he was gone, he gave me a busted lip and a bruised leg.

Corvell shook his head with pity. "This is getting old. He should be tired of doing this mess by now."

I sighed hopelessly. "Yeah, you would think."

"We could always kill him Neph," Nikki said, looking up

from her cell phone momentarily.

"Kill?" Corvell asked incredulously. He spun around on his barstool to give Nikki wide eyes. "I know you ain't talking about killing somebody. Aren't you against violence?"

"Not when it comes to him," Nikki turned up her nose. "I'm sick of Marcos."

Corvell spun back around to look at me sympathetically. "We need Ms. Thang here to get sick of his ass."

"I am," I told them quietly.

Nikki looked up from her phone again and snorted a sarcastic laugh. "That didn't sound very convincing."

"I am," I reiterated. "I just don't know how to get rid of him."

Nikki mumbled, "Antifreeze."

Changing the subject, Corvell asked, "Well what about dude you been talking to?"

"What dude?" This made Nikki put her phone completely down.

The thought of Blake made me smile but caused me to sadden. I had been ignoring him for the past few days. I just didn't want to be bothered because I was too busy sulking. Not only that, but I came to the conclusion that I was wasting his time. Besides, I didn't need to add to my troubles by inviting someone new into my tumultuous life. I couldn't be anything more but a telephone conversation for him anyway.

"I was talking to this guy from the dating thing," I said without a care.

"What do you mean *was*?" Corvell asked.

"I don't need to keep talking to him," I replied.

"He knows your situation?" Nikki asked.

"Nope," I answered.

Nikki hopped off her barstool and slung her purse over her shoulder. "Keep him on the side or something."

Corvell asked, "You leaving now?"

"Yeah," Nikki grinned. "Going to this barbecue with Trevor."

"And why couldn't you invite anybody?" Corvell countered.

Nikki screwed her face in taken aback gesture. "Why would I invite you and it's supposed to be me meeting Trevor's family. What I look like bringing my pet friend along?"

"A pet friend?" Corvell feigned insult.

I shook my head and laughed at them. Corvell hopped off of his barstool too. "Well let me get up outta here. Neph, you sure you don't wanna come out with me?"

I nodded. "I'm positive. But y'all have fun and be careful."

All three of us exchanged farewell hugs, and then I walked them to the front door. When they left, I was alone, and this big house seemed so empty. Although Yanna decided to stay behind, she went to my sister's house with Lailani. Ada was gone spending the holiday with her own family.

As I looked around my home, I knew there was so much for me to be thankful for, but I was empty. I needed something to fill that void.

I went to my phone, and I text Blake: **hey**

It took several minutes, but he responded.

Blake: **hey**

Me: **I wanna meet**

Blake: **Now?**

Me: **not right now because I'm sure you're celebrating with family**

Blake: **when and are you sure?**

Me: **I wanna take things to another level.**

Blake: **What do you mean?**

Me: **I hadn't been intimate in a while**

Blake: **Answer this question first and please be honest. Are you still with your husband?**

Me: **No**

Blake: **I don't think you're telling the truth**

Me: **why do you care? I'm trying to have sex, and you're asking questions. I thought that's what you men wanted**

Blake: **I care because you're still with your husband and I don't want those problems. And don't put all of us men in the same box**

I was losing my patience. Me: **Can we meet or what?**

Blake: **No. I'm sure your husband wouldn't appreciate it. Do you think sleeping with me will take away whatever he done to you?**

I rolled my eyes. He really was like my therapist now.

Me: **He's a woman beater and that's all he's ever**

done these whole 19 years. He don't love me. He never has. He loves his other baby mama more than he do me. And for the life of me I can't figure out what I've ever done to deserve this life with him. I'm miserable.

The angry tears spilled over my bottom lids, rolled down my cheeks and landed on the screen of my phone.

Blake: **Do you hate him?**

Me: **Yes and I wish he would have a stroke and die!**

Blake: **I'm sorry that you have gone through that.**

Me: **Yeah I am too**

Blake: **I can't go to that next level with you. Not as long as you're still a married woman and you're with him. Once you've taken care of that situation, then we'll see where things can go between us. I wish you the best of luck and take care.**

This was just great! I can't win for anything.

Me: **You have yourself a good life. Be blessed!**

I was pissed about Blake. For some reason, I was starting to believe he was going to be my knight in shining armor. I was so disappointed. And if that wasn't enough, when Marcos and the kids returned a few days later, he had the nerves to be in a good mood.

"You didn't miss me?" he asked in a teasing tone. I was sitting on the sofa in the den, and he had come around blocking my view of the television.

I cut my eyes at him. When had I ever miss him?

"Why you gotta look so mean?"

Did he just ask me that? Wait! Don't he remember that he gave me a busted lip before he left?

I guess he forgot about all of that. He leaned down and proceeded to kiss me, but I pushed him away.

Insulted, he asked, "You really don't miss me huh?"

I shook my head and continued to focus on the television.

I don't know what he had been smoking while he was in Columbia, but this was so out of character for him. He began kissing me on my neck, nibbling at my ears, and nipping me here and there with little teasing bites. It was too affectionate coming from him, and it was making me uncomfortable.

I pushed him away. "Will you stop?"

He sat down beside me, and in a more serious tone, he said, "For some reason these last couple of days you've been really on my mind. I couldn't wait to get back just to see your face. I've been wanting to make love to you. And—"

My laughter interrupted him. I looked at him and said, "Make love?"

"Why is that funny?"

I waved him off shaking my head with skepticism. "Marcos, stop playing with me."

"A man can't miss his wife?"

"Why would you miss me? You've never missed me. Why now? Did burying your grandmother give you some great epiphany?"

He sat there as if he was pondering the thought.

I couldn't resist laughing again.

Hesitantly, Marcos said, "Let's work things out."

"Like counseling?" I asked for clarity.

He shook his head. "You know how I feel about that counseling shit. We can do this ourselves."

"We would need a mediator because as soon as I say or do something that you don't like, then I'll get smacked. No thanks Marcos," I said. By the end of my statement, I had grown angry. The idea of he and I working things out was absurd especially if we were doing it strictly by his terms.

"So you wanna keep things the way they are?" he asked.

"Minus you hitting on me, yeah," I answered sarcastically.

He stared at me for a few seconds. For a minute there I thought I detected hurt and dejection in his face, but it was quickly replaced with vexation. He abruptly got up and walked out of the den.

I thought I had gotten rid of him but much to my surprise, he didn't go anywhere. I wanted him to leave like he normally did. I didn't like when he was home anymore. I know that seemed backward because a part of me wanted him to have the desire to be home; at least for the kids more. But for me, I could do without him.

After my time with the kids that night, I retired to my bedroom. I ignored Marcos lying in bed as I prepared for bed. When I finally got in bed, I still ignored him. I think he liked it better that way. If I ignored him, then I had to keep the charade up when he attacked me aggressively stripping me of my clothes.

I didn't assist him in any way. I had to pretend that I didn't want it. I didn't. I rather it had been someone else;

someone new. But honestly, I enjoyed sex when he took it. Maybe it was the way he had conditioned me to be. That's why when he used words like "make love" I think it's funny. Marcos hadn't been gentle with me since the beginning of our sex life.

Skipping the joys of foreplay, he got right to it. Keeping me on my back, he roughly snatched my leg over his, and he dug into me while on his side. I hated responding to him, but the way he was stroking me sent little shivers throughout my body. My breasts ached and were begging for attention. Seeing me massage them prompted him to start rubbing on them. He even took the closest one in his mouth.

I moaned accidentally. I bit down on my bottom lip to keep from doing it again, but it just came out as forced groans. Shit! What was into him? I would have asked, but his mouth found its way to mine. Before I knew it, we were in an intense lip lock. It made my stomach quiver, and my pussy convulsed around him. That caused him to moan into my mouth, and at that moment I realized sex with me was actually enjoyable for him. I used to think it was just something to get him a nut, but I guess he did enjoy me sexually.

When he began to rub on my clit as his dick massaged my insides, I began speaking in tongues. He could ask me to do anything right now, and I would oblige.

"You love me Neph?"

I moaned and nodded my head.

"Tell me," he panted into my ear.

I tried to look at him, but my eyes kept rolling around. I managed a weak, "I love you."

Did I or was it the sex? Did I love Marcos? As always, I was torn. I wanted to love this man, but I also hoped he got ran over by an industrial size tractor.

If I could still get pregnant, I'm sure I would have gotten pregnant. The way he came seemed like he dumped a pound of semen in me. It took a lot out of him as if he had been letting that build up. Within seconds of cumming he was snoring in my ear; literally snoring in my ear. He hadn't moved he was still at my side with his softened member still inside me.

I wanted to think about what just happened, but even I was too tired to keep my eyes open for much longer.

———————

Lillian was super excited about this therapy session. I wasn't. As a matter of fact, I was beginning to think it was stupid and a waste of time. However, I agreed to it. So here I was sitting in Lillian's office waiting for our third party.

Lillian was clicking around on her computer when a knock came to the door.

"She's here," she said with glee as she got up to greet the person.

I waited quietly until the person came fully into the office and the door was closed.

Before taking a seat, Lillian introduced us. "Nephia meet Bless. Bless this is Nephia. I'm so glad that you agree to do this."

Pleasantly, Bless stretched her hand out to me. "It's nice to meet you."

I absently took her hand and studied her face. I knew this woman. To be sure I asked, "Aren't you related to Special K?"

Bless looked clueless.

"Kennedi," I stated.

"Oh!" She laughed as it dawned on her. "I forgot that's what she has people calling her. Yeah, that's my niece."

"She's a student at the music and dance school," I told her. "I'm an instructor there, but my husband's family own it."

Again, Bless was delighted, and her eyes grew in wonderment. "Okay! You're Mrs. Beauchamp's daughter-in-law. Kennedi loves that place. Her cousins go there as well. They all love it."

Observing Bless, even more, I could see the family resemblance. Bless didn't possess the same chocolate complexion as Kennedi but she did have the same rounded babydoll face with big slanted eyes.

Lillian interjected, "Well isn't this great."

Now I had become curious. Lillian suggested that I meet with another patient of hers who has had her own bouts of domestic violence. She felt like I should hear this woman's story and hopefully it would somehow have an impact on me. The times I've seen Bless at the school, she never came off as some miserable broken woman. She seemed to be full of spirit just as much as her niece.

No more time was wasted as Bless sat down in a chair across from me and began to tell her story of her ex-husband. The last straw for her was when he had stabbed her multiple times. She pointed out every single slightly keloid scar adorning her body in various places that he left behind. She went on to tell me how she struggled with her decisions to work with the courts to have him put away for a long time. She said a lot of it had to do with their two sons being without their father. Fortunately for her, she had a twin brother that was there for her.

Bless even told me a story about her brother's ordeal with domestic violence. He lost the woman he was about to marry at the hands of her daughter's father on the day they were supposed to marry.

Although she gave me a lot to think about, there was a numbness over me that I couldn't explain. I mean my heart went out to them and everything they suffered through. But for me...I just felt like this was my fate. There was no saving me. Besides, I didn't have it in me to leave or put Marcos away. I appreciated what Bless and Lillian were trying to do, but I didn't leave this session with no more of a plan of action than I had before. I would simply continue to pray for a natural disaster to wipe Marcos off the face of this earth.

Chapter 17: *Back to the present*

As we rushed into the labor and delivery department of Vanderbilt, I could sense that Bleu was nervous. The four of us entered Shana's hospital room. She looked weary and frightened.

Shana's mother Claire rolled her eyes at the sight of Beverly. The tension was almost immediate. Since the news of Bleu having a baby on the way was made known to everyone, Beverly was the only one that remained skeptical and made sure everyone knew where she stood on the matter. I had gotten used to the idea of being a grandmother, so I wasn't given Shana a bunch of flack. Beverly was adamant that Shana and her mother were scheming.

Ignoring Claire and not bothering to speak, Beverly asked Shana, "How dilated are you now?"

"Five and a half," Shana said meekly.

"You already got your epidural?" I asked.

Shana nodded shocked.

I took a seat on the built-in bench next to the picture window in the room. "So we wait. Oh excuse my manners; how are you, Ms. Roberts?"

Claire smiled, "I'm fine. Just waiting for this baby. How are you?"

"I'm good," I said. I looked at my sons, one nervous and worried as hell; the other one worried for his brother. "You two sit down."

Beverly cut her eyes at me. I shook my head and laughed lightly. I already knew what was going on through her head.

She didn't need me fraternizing with the enemy.

Beverly asked, "So did you call the other little boy?"

I knew it was coming. And I knew this was the only reason she insisted on accompanying us.

"Nana," Bleu frowned.

Beverly placed her hand on her hip, "Don't Nana me. You ain't the only one that might be the father."

"He is," Shana said lowly keeping her head down. She refused to look at Beverly. I didn't blame her. Beverly's grandeur presence was still just as intimidating as it was eighteen years ago.

"Didn't you say you didn't know at first?" Beverly asked.

"Beverly," I called out. "Not right now. Don't stress her out while she's in labor. It's not good for the baby."

Bleu shot me a look letting me know his grandmother was getting on his nerves.

Beverly sat down beside me fluttering her lashes and perching her lips tight.

As Bleu spoke softly to Shana, I could see that he was nothing like his father. I sensed he had a genuine concern for Shana. I couldn't remember not one delivery of mine that Marcos was there for me comforting me. There was always something much more important than the pain I was in.

Claire asked with a pleasant smile, "How's Marcos?"

"He's recovering fine," I replied. Actually, I didn't know how he was doing. He had just been discharged from the hospital and was home now. Either Lailani or I would be taking him to all of his doctor's and therapy appointments. I wasn't looking forward to it. I barely paid attention to the discharge orders from his doctor when he left the hospital. All I know is Marcos was seeing every specialist there was in the medical field.

Since being home, Marcos kept to himself in our bedroom. I slept in Marcena's old room since she was gone to Washington, D.C. for college. Ada and Lailani communicated with him more than I did. The kids would creep into the room to check on him. Yanna said he was weird now. I don't know why but that gave me the giggles when she reported back to me. But he was weird. If I went in the room, his eyes would follow me, but he wouldn't say anything. I think losing a leg has taken a big chunk of his spirit. He wasn't the same anymore. I could see the devastation and anger in his eyes.

It serves him right, and I didn't feel any sympathy for him at all. He called himself trying to hurt me even more than he has ever before. After that therapy session with Bless, I went home, and I told Marcos what I thought of him. I wanted to die, but I was too much of a coward to commit suicide. I figure I'd get him mad enough to do it for me. So I expressed freely and with confidence how I felt about him. And I went about it as hurtful as I could. But he didn't do anything to me that day. He disappeared for a few days. When he returned, he came back uglier than ever.

You know what? Thinking back on it, as I sit in this girl's delivery room, I think I messed up. When Marcos came back from Columbia, he was different. He spoke in a way that threw me off. I didn't take him seriously because I didn't think he was capable of wanting anything different between us. What if he was serious and my rejection caused him to treat me worse than before? Why am I rationalizing this in my head though? If he truly desired to have a better relationship, a better marriage with me, then why resort to mistreating me? And when I say he got worse, he really got worse. You see the shit he pulled at the boys' birthday party? Cold and very menacing, just to hurt me.

An hour and a half later Shana gave birth to a seven-pound eight-ounce baby girl. Since she was white, the baby looked white. Beverly refused to see any resemblance to the family. I could see it. Beverly had to admit though, the baby girl was beautiful. It was official; I was a grandmother.

———————

I missed talking to Blake. I needed male interaction. I was feeling lonely again. I could think of a lot of things to be doing besides chauffeuring Mr. Cripple everywhere.

"Okay Marcos, I'm gonna show you a series of photo cards, and I want you to tell me what they are," said the speech therapist. She was a middle-aged brunette woman with a pleasant smile. Her name was Jean.

She held up a picture of a red ball. Marcos looked at it and didn't bother to give her a reply.

Jean sort of waved it in the air. "C'mon. I know you know what this is. Say it, Marcos."

He looked away from her as if he was defeated. I shook my head because even in his vulnerable condition he still wanted to be stubborn.

I think he saw me shaking my head because he threw me a hateful stare. I wanted to laugh at him, but the people in the office probably wouldn't think that was nice of me. I returned my attention back to Candy Crush Soda Saga on my iPad.

"Do you wanna skip this one?"

I don't know whether Marcos wanted to skip it or not, but there was more silence.

"What about this one?"

I looked up and saw she was holding a picture of a school bus.

Marcos eyes nervously shot over to me. I waited to see if he would answer this one. He looked at the card then back at me. Why was he looking at me?

Before I could put my head back down, I heard his voice come out in a raspy whisper.

"R-r-ride," he stammered.

Ride? I scrunched up my nose to keep from laughing.

Jean shrieked with glee. "Yes! You do ride on this. Now we're getting somewhere. What about this?"

She held up a picture of a dog.

With uncertainty, Marcos strained to say, "Barking...barking."

Wait a minute now. I missed something. I was aware that when Marcos first awakened from his coma that he was dealing with apraxia of speech which was common for stroke patients. During his time at the hospital, I was told he began speaking again, so his silence at home was voluntary. I was beginning to see why he kept quiet.

I sat there in amazement as he struggled with recalling the actual name of what was on the card. He said words that were close to it or had something to do with it. Some cards he didn't have anything at all. When he got back to the red ball, he finally referred to it as "round."

I finally had to ask Jean, "Why can he not say what these things are?"

She happily explained, "Marcos suffer from Broca's aphasia. It's a speech impairment that makes it difficult for him to recall words. He knows what it is but the part of his brain where word association is stored is sort of closed off to him. It's hard for him to retrieve the exact word."

"How long will this go on?" I asked. I could feel Marcos staring a hole in me.

Jean shrugged. "It's something that he'll struggle with for a while. But with consistent therapy, his ability to communicate should improve over time. With the right amount of support at home, his willingness to overcome, and therapy Marcos can be his old self in no time."

His old self? Did this woman know who Marcos' old self was?

After the session was over, I stood at the check out counter taking care of the bill and making his next appointment. Marcos sat down in the office's waiting area.

Jean came up to me with her pleasant smile. Her eyes darted over to Marcos then back at me. "Your husband has been through a lot, and I know all of this is new to you and the rest of the family. One of the best things for him on his road to recovery is family support. And you guys have been doing an excellent job of doing so, but I noticed when you're with him, he's more hesitant and unsure of himself. Do you know why that could be?"

I shook my head as I took my bank card from the receptionist and tucked it away in my purse. "I didn't realize he was doing that."

"Yeah, I really noticed it today. He kept looking over at you. Maybe that's something you could talk to him about. Other than that, he's made so much progress; a long way from when I first visited him in the hospital a few weeks ago."

I looked over at him. I found it eerie for him to be staring right back at me. I took care of everything at the counter. I went over to him and said, "I'll go get the car and pull it up to the front of the building."

He shook his head reaching for his crutches. He stood up on his own and balanced himself. Once he felt confident, he proceeded to walk. His gait was off as he walked on his temporary prosthesis but that's what the crutches were for. I had to give it to him, he was determined to walk around as close to normal as possible.

"So you wanna walk?" I asked just to be sure.

He nodded as he walked ahead of me. I wouldn't argue with him.

Once we were secured inside of the car, I asked, "You want something to eat?"

He nodded. I started the car and began driving.

"You wanna stop by your uncle's? He asked about you the other day. He hadn't been able to make it over to the house since you've been home."

Marcos shook his head and focused on the scenery outside his window. I could see that he wasn't in the mood to be bothered.

"Marcos, there's no need in avoiding everyone. You can't stay in the bedroom for the rest of your life. Is that what you're trying to do?"

Of course, he didn't say anything, but when I glanced over at him, his brow was furrowed with irritation. I think I discovered my new purpose: to get on his nerves as much as I can.

————————

Later that night, I decided to have a talk with Marcos. I walked into our bedroom while he was tending to his leg as the doctors had instructed him how to. When he saw me a look of embarrassment waved over his face, and he covered himself with the comforter on the bed.

I sat on the edge of the bed beside him and looked him sympathetically, "You don't have to feel embarrassed or ashamed. Is there anything I can do for you?"

He just stared at me.

I sort of dropped my shoulders down in defeat. I began speaking, "You know, at first I didn't care about what you were going through. As a matter of fact, I had very evil thoughts and wanted you to die. I admit that I had tuned out everything the doctors explained about all of your conditions. But I don't know...seeing you today really trying kind of did something to me."

I paused and gathered my thoughts.

"At first I thought this was the perfect time for us to legally separate. I had seen this cute little place for rent online. It's only a three-bedroom, but I figured the kids could have lived in both houses. I'm sure Bleu and Azul would have wanted to stay here most of the time. Remi and Yanna would definitely wanna come with me. I'm not sure about Stormi and Raiyne though."

"No."

I was shocked. He said that very clear and with no hesitation. There was even some authority in his tone.

I sighed and averted my eyes down to the floor. "Marcos, I've spent more than half of my life being unhappy with you. And all I ever wanted was for you to love me. Not love me because I was the mother of your kids but love *me*. Love me because you felt you had no purpose if you couldn't. Love because it felt good. Love me because you wanted me to experience the beauty of love..."

I knew I was going to get emotional although I tried my best to hold my tears back.

"And in a way, I used to feel indebted to you because you came along and removed me, my sister, and my mama from a dire situation. I was so grateful for that. So I loved you. And whether you know this or not, I always believed that there was a good person inside of you. You let him come out from time to time, but for the most part, you treated me like garbage. And I never knew why. I spent all of these years trying to figure out why you hated me. What did I do? I mean, all I ever tried to do was prove to you that I was here and that I loved you. I was willing to be whatever you needed me to be. You didn't have to beat me to make me stay or do any of that. You didn't have to put fear in me to make me stay."

I looked up at him through tear-blurred eyes and saw silent tears rolling down his cheeks.

"I was your wife! I was gonna stay regardless. You didn't have to do me...," I started crying. I had to wait a few seconds to gather myself. I continued, "And now I'm faced with having to take care of you; get you back to your old self. But your old self doesn't love me. And I'd rather not be around when he gets back. But because I know I still love you—as much as I hate that I do, I know I do—I'm willing to help you get back to your old self. Just know, that I have to move on."

"No," he objected again. His mouth opened as his brain searched for the correct words, but the task was proving to be frustrating. I hated to see him struggle and it seemed like the more stressed he was, the harder it was for him.

"Don't try to speak. I just wanted you to listen," I told him as I got up. He reached out to me, but in my mind, I thought he wanted to attack me. My immediate reaction was to jump back.

When he saw that, he looked at me with sorrow and defeat. He was hurt. As much as I wanted to take joy in his pain, I just couldn't. I wasn't built that way.

Taking a risk, before I walked out of the room, I leaned down and placed a kiss on his forehead. "I love you."

"I don't know Neph," Corvell said. He observed Marcos working through his physical therapy session with the therapist in our den. "It looks like that nigga really trying to make a full recovery. And when he do, I would not wanna be you."

I actually smiled at Corvell's statement. "I don't think I have anything to worry about."

"What's up with this new attitude?" he asked with a hint of amusement.

I shrugged. I don't think what I was feeling was a change of attitude. It was more like I was coming into a peacefulness that I had never experienced before. It felt good being released from the hold people had over you. Furthermore, it felt even better knowing that someone else was at your mercy and you consciously decided that continuing to treat them with kindness would prevail. So yes, lately I was feeling a little triumphant.

Bleu came running through the den and by the kitchen yelling at me at the same time, "Shana's here!"

Before I knew it, the rest of the kids had scrambled through the kitchen and den meeting Shana, the baby, and Claire before they could fully make it through the house.

Between me, Corvell, Ada, Lailani, and the kids, baby Lauryn was the star for the evening.

"He's gon' be a real good daddy," Ada murmured under her breath. "Thank God he won't be nothing like his own daddy and that damn granddaddy of his."

I chuckled because I thought the same thing as I took note of how Bleu cared for Lauryn. He didn't seem scared at all. It was almost as if it came naturally to him.

Ada looked over at Marcos. "He lookin' right pitiful. God sho do have a way of making a person be still and seein' thangs a lil diff'rently."

Is that what happened to Marcos? Did he have a different perspective on life?

Since the house had become lively, the physical therapist cut Marcos' therapy short. As soon as he did, Marcos quietly escaped. I followed behind him undetected. He went into the bedroom straight to the master bathroom. Then there was silence and no movement.

I moved in closer to see what he was doing. He stood before our double sink vanity with his head lowered in deep thought. His hands rested on the counter and arms locked holding him up. He stood with most of his weight on his good leg.

Finally lifting his head up he immediately noticed me standing in the doorway through the mirror's reflection. I don't know what bothered me the most; him crying or my heart dropping at the sight of him crying. It didn't just drop, but it went out to him.

It's not in me to be evil. I went to him and did what I've always done: I loved him.

We stood there holding each other for dear life, and I let him cry while trying not to cry and remain strong for him. I wasn't doing a good job of it. Talking through the tears, I said, "We're gonna get through this. I promise we will."

He pulled back and tried to say something. All he could say was the word "don't" as he shook his head. Next, he pointed to himself, then to me emphasizing with "don't."

I knew what he was trying to say. He was trying to tell me that he didn't deserve me. And before I could respond to that, he managed to say, "Sorry."

I knew right then that I wasn't going anywhere. I also knew that things between us were about to be different. I used to hate that I loved him so much. I wanted to not love him. Sure I hated the things he had done and the way he mistreated me, but I was still an advocate for change. All I ever wanted was for him to love me in the same way that I loved him. I believe that moment had come.

Chapter 18: *Four weeks later...*

I held Marcos' hand and looked at him sleeping. He looked so peaceful. I think he was at peace. I think he had come to terms with the fact that he knew he hadn't been the best man he could have possibly been. He also accepted that what happened to him was a direct consequence of it. I tried to tell him I didn't agree with that, but he made me be quiet by placing his hand over my mouth and shaking his head. He waved his hand dismissively and shrugged with a smile. That was his way of saying he was okay with it.

Beverly waltzed into the room like she always did as if she was the Queen of Sheba.

"I got here as soon as I could," she said holding out her hands to examine them. She started rambling on and on. "I was in the middle of getting my mani-pedi when you called me earlier. The first young lady doing my manicure didn't seem to know what she was doing. I told them I couldn't have no one practicing on me. Kayla, the girl who usually does my nails, wasn't there. So—"

"Beverly," I said softly.

She continued to talk a mile a minute. "I agreed to let that young girl give it a try. I should have known better. She looked as if she had just gotten off the boat and didn't know a lick of English."

I tried again, "Beverly."

"Yes dear," she said walking over to the other side of Marcos. "How's he doing? Andrés should be here any minute. I just spoke to him."

"Beverly, Marcos left us about an hour ago."

A stunned Beverly looked at me then at her son lying in the hospital bed. It finally registered that all of the machinery was off and disconnected. The room was quiet.

Beverly shook her head in disbelief. "No. He's not gone yet." She covered her mouth in shock as she started to cry. "Is he Neph?"

The tears began to fall from my eyes once again confirming the answer to her question. I had been sitting at his bedside for more than an hour. As a matter of fact, I had been here every day for hours at a time ever since he had been admitted a little over a week before. It all happened so fast, and it seemed like it was out of the blue.

I was able to spend a little over two weeks with my husband. He wasn't his old self, and it didn't look like he would have ever been that person again. And it wasn't just about him being an abusive man. His physical self would have never returned to who he used to be.

I think out of the entire nineteen years of being with him, these past few weeks I loved him the most. We laughed a lot with the kids. Yanna had become his little guardian and catered to him. I think his death was going to have the biggest effect on her out of all of the kids. Like me, she was losing someone she was just getting in her life.

Like I said, things took a sudden change for the worst. We went to his appointment with the nephrologist, and the results of in-office diagnostic tests alarmed the doctor right away. Marcos' kidneys had failed as a result of his PKD, and his toxin levels were through the roof. Sepsis set in quickly, and it progressed rapidly within days. Everything started shutting down. If he had complained at the first onset of symptoms, then maybe he would still be with us. I knew he had seemed weaker and it seemed as if he was overexerting himself during physical therapy. I'm not sure if I chose to ignore it because it was a tell-tale sign of what was to come or if I dismissed it as no big deal. Whichever the reason, Marcos didn't want me worrying.

He held on as long as he could. He took his last breath an hour ago.

I didn't want to let go of his hand, but I had to comfort Beverly. Jovelyn and Lailani both entered the room right as Beverly lost it and had a breakdown. Hospital staff responded to assist in calming her down.

With swollen red eyes, Jovelyn walked over to me. "Have you told the kids yet?"

I shook my head. I wasn't ready to tell them. I wish I didn't have to.

"Go ahead and tell Marcena so she can be on her way home," Jovelyn said.

I took my phone out and sent Marcena a text: **He's gone, come home**

Seconds later my phone was ringing. It was Marcena. I couldn't talk to her, so I passed the phone to Jovelyn. My sister told her again that her father, Marcos Delgado Beauchamp had passed away. I could faintly hear Marcena's hysterical cries coming from the phone.

After Jovelyn ended the call with her, she passed me my phone back. She asked, "What do you need me to do?"

I shrugged. "Nothing right now."

My phone began ringing. It was Azul. I answered it trying to sound normal. "Hello?"

"Is he gone for real?" my son cried into the phone.

Dammit! Marcena must have called or text her siblings. I sighed, "Yes, he's gone."

I didn't know what to say to comfort him, so I listened to Azul crying into the phone. I could hear someone in the background asking him what the matter was. The next thing I knew Bleu was on the phone in disbelief. They told me they were leaving school right then.

After ending the call with them, I debated if I should let the others finish their day in school or go ahead and get them early. I sent Corvell, Chrissy, Nikki, Gogo, and Quan a group text.

I thought back to Ada and what she said. *"God sho do have a way of making a person be still and seein' thangs a lil diffrently."*

He did. I love you, Marcos.

A month later....

It was the Adele Beauchamp School of Music and Theatre's winter performance. This was one of the events I always looked forward to. All of the kids participated in some type of skit, dance, music—something. I loved it. These kids were remarkably talented.

This year, I decided to do an impromptu contemporary solo dance to *Thinking Out Loud* by Ed Sheeran, but it was performed live by one of the students, Grace Masters as she played on an acoustic guitar. It was dedicated to Marcos.

I didn't think it would be so difficult to actually get through it. I had heard Grace sing this song so many times, but this night it did something different to me. I was overwhelmed with so many emotions. I realized I was angry. It wasn't fair. I was so mad at Marcos. It seemed as though he gave me what I always wanted and in that same moment of time, he had taken it away.

I had been going through some of Marcos' belongings after his burial, trying to find all of the good things about him for me to hold onto. And in the box that held the things recovered from his car accident was a small notepad. I flipped through the tattered pages until I got to a page with a bunch of random scribbling and words jotted down. When I paid more attention to it, I realized that these were random thoughts of Marcos' in his handwriting. Circled several times, he made a note: *Have Neph to make me appt w/therapist.* Then there was a little list: *work on being a better man, a better father, brother, son, and husband.* My name was in all caps by itself and circled many times. There were also random notes jotted such as *Call Lil Don for twins party, call Steve, f/u with doctor.*

This piece of paper confirmed for me that Marcos was aware that he was sick. And according to the paper he knew before the twins' birthday party. Steve was his accountant. After Marcos' funeral, Steve met with me to go over all of the financial securities Marcos had in place for us. So Marcos knew what was to come. But I think what touched me the most was when I flipped to the next page.

Nephia,

I know you hate me. I hate me too. But

Neph

I'm sorry

I love you. I love you. I love you...

He had listed all of our names, mine and the kids, down in a row. He misspelled Raiyne's name though. He never wanted to put the "i" in her name.

I just stared at the paper and cried.

I was sad. I was also happy. I grieved Marcos' death for two weeks. I isolated myself. I broke some things. I even called and cussed Terra out just because. Then I called back to ask if Brittani could come over to the house.

Once I got all of that out I was able to make some peace with everything. But where do I go from here? I still had a lot of healing to do. Not so much as dealing with my ability to give love another chance but removing the insecurities that were associated with the turbulent relationship I once had with Marcos. I hope I wasn't too messed up for the next man.

The rest of the night was astounding. I couldn't have asked for a more perfect program. I was proud of everyone. But even with my touching solo, Special K still stole the show during her group's performance. She had a natural way of performing that pulled an audience in. Her facial expression alone put on a show. Her confidence was enough for ten kids. There was absolutely nothing shy about that girl.

Speaking of, Kennedi and Bless walked up to me during the after-show reception.

Sweetly, Bless said, "I just wanted to come over to say hi."

I smiled, "It's nice seeing you. Your niece did an amazing job."

"Well so did you. You and the rest of the staff do a wonderful job with all of the kids, but that dance you did earlier—Oh!" Bless clutched her chest as she sighed. "It moved me to tears."

"Tears?" Kennedi questioned with skepticism. "Tears Tee-tee?"

"Oh hush," Bless said playfully tapping her shoulder.

"Did Daddy cry too?" Kennedi asked. "You know that's Daddy song. Daddy listen to that song all the time. He had it playing over and over one day. I was like dang! I said 'Daddy, if you don't stop that song I'm gonna think out loud upside yo' head.' I sure did."

Bless said, "You did not tell your daddy that!"

"I did too. Ask him," Kennedi said. She was so serious in her tone that it was cute.

"Bebe!" Bless called. She waved to someone that wasn't in my view just yet. She turned to me and asked me, "You haven't met my brother yet, have you?"

"Daddy hardly ever come to the school," Kennedi stated.

Bless grasped Kennedi's daddy's arm to pull him over and said, "Bebe, this is Nephia, one of Kennedi's instructors here at the school."

I was already wearing a smile to greet the man, but my smile broadened, even more, when I was staring at a very familiar face. A little thrown off, I said, "Hey."

Bebe returned the same giddy grin and said, "Hey."

Oblivious to our existing knowledge of one another, Bless went on to say, "Bebe, this is also the one that I was telling you about."

"Yeah, I kinda figured that out," he said not taking his eyes off of me.

Then it finally registered to me. If Bebe was the brother that Bless spoke of during that therapy session, then he's the one that lost his wife-to-be the day they were supposed to get married. It made sense. I wasn't even mad anymore.

Kennedi had to prove that she told her daddy to stop listening to that song. Bebe confirmed that she was telling the truth. Another student Kennedi's age pulled her away and Bless had to go to the ladies' room which left me and Bebe standing there.

"So your name isn't Blake?" I asked.

"No, it's Blyss, but people call me Bebe. Blake was short for my last name."

Kennedi Blakemore! Of course!

"Zero five two four?" I asked curiously. I think I already had the answer.

"If Bless told you the story about her brother that was supposed to get married, that's the date it was supposed to happen."

I looked up at him with empathy. "I'm sorry."

"I'm good," he said. He then asked, "So your husband recently died?"

I nodded.

"It's funny you dedicated that dance to him, and the whole time I was watching you, I couldn't help but think about Miki. She wanted to do this. She talked about being a dancer. I wanted to..."

His voice trailed off, and I could tell his mind was going back in time. He was still hurting over the loss of his wife-to-be. It was evident.

"Is your heart still broken?" I asked.

"Something like that," he said quietly. He then stated, "You know they're iffy."

"What?"

"Broken hearts; they can't be trusted. Today they tell you one thing, but tomorrow it could be something else."

I laughed softly in revelation. "And one minute they love to hate you and the next they hate to love you."

Our eyes locked onto one another's knowingly. Something existed between us. It was intangible, but it was there.

Bebe finally broke our odd silence and said, "My number is still the same. I mean this isn't under the circumstances in which I wanted to hear from you again, but if you need an empathetic ear, I'm here."

"I'll keep that in mind," I smiled.

He smiled back. "And you are so much more beautiful in person."

I blushed of course. I reciprocated the compliment. "And you're very very handsome in person."

"Call me...when you're ready. Okay?"

I nodded. He sorta did this reassuring nod as he walked away. I couldn't take my eyes off of him as he went to talk to Grace's father.

"Bitch, who is that?" Corvell asked as he came and stood beside me.

On the other side of me stood Nikki. She said, "Is he a prospect?"

I turned to face them both with the brightest smile. "That is Special K's daddy. And remember the friend I was talking to from that dating app?"

Nikki looked at me as if she didn't believe me. "Why you playing?"

"Him?" Corvell asked in disbelief.

I nodded. "That's him."

"Well, what's up with that?" Corvell wanted to know.

"Nothing," I simply said.

"That ain't how y'all was looking. It's something," Nikki pointed out.

"It's too soon," I said.

Corvell said, "Well honey, when too soon is over with, you let that be the first on your to-do list. And I mean to do! Baby boom!"

I shook my head. Corvell was forever a mess.

Bebe and I had some things in common. He and I both had a taste of the same struggles. He knew domestic violence in one way, and I knew it in another. Clearly, the death of his loved one had a profound effect on him as the death of my loved one did for me. We were both broken yet repairable. It would take time. And as I stated to Corvell and Nikki, it was too soon, or so that's what I had convinced myself.

To my surprise, later that night a text message from Blake popped up on my phone: **The man/woman who removes a mountain begins by carrying away small**

stones...Things seem kinda tough now, but I promise, you will make it through.

I smiled uncontrollably. I text back: **Thank you!**

And now my journey begins...

About the Author

Ada Henderson brings her imagination to life as she writes amazing urban romance fiction under the pseudonym Ivy Symone. Writing has always been a passion of hers even before she realized that's exactly what it was: passion!

The urge to put daydreams to paper began for her at the tender age of ten. The impulse to write was sporadic over the years; but as an adult she picked writing back up, and it served as a therapeutic outlet for her. It wasn't until late 2013 that her mother encouraged her to get published.

Ivy's first debut novel was Why Should I Love You. After that, came Why Should I Love You 2 & 3, Secrets Between Her Thighs 1 & 2, Never Trust A Broken Heart, Crush 1, 2, & 3, Hate To Love You, Stay, If You're Willing, Bad Habitzz, and The Bed We Made. Ivy humbly received two AAMBC awards: 2015 Ebook of the Year and 2015 Urban Book of the Year for her phenomenal Crush series.

She currently resides in Nashville, TN with two of four children in her home. When Ivy is not reading or writing, she's enjoying cooking, watching horror movies all day long, and spending quality time with her friends and family.